STOLEN VOICES

Published by Lobster Press™
1620 Sherbrooke Street West, Suites C & D
Montréal, Québec   H3H 1C9
Tel. (514) 904-1100 • Fax (514) 904-1101 • www.lobsterpress.com

Publisher: Alison Fripp
Editors: Alison Fripp & Karen Li
Editorial Assistants: Meghan Nolan & Penny Smart
Graphic Design & Production: Tammy Desnoyers

Library and Archives Canada Cataloguing in Publication

Davidson, Ellen Dee, 1954-
        Stolen voices / Ellen Dee Davidson.

ISBN 1-897073-16-X

        I. Title.

PS3604.A93S76 2005   813'.6   C2005-901047-9

Printed and bound in Canada.

To Francine Tuft Peterson for seeing and believing in my
Talent when I didn't know I had one, with love and gratitude
for bringing me so many blessings. To the kids who read and
helped me with this book: Gabriel, Renee, Victor, Ann Marie,
Fiona, Michaela, Alisha, Luke, Mariposa, Hannah, Jessica, and
Michelle, and her bunny, Butterball. To Lorraine and Xande for
brainstorming and Grandma Laura for support. To Writers by
the Sea: Barbara Kelly, Mary Nethery, Natasha Wing, and Pam
Service for generous help with revisions. To the other artists
and writers in my life who give me the courage and heart to go
on: Annette Holland, Joan Dunning, Margaret Draper, and Kerri
Mabee. To my healing and visionary friends: Marina Pierce,
Maya Cooper, Joan Dixon, and Marna Utman. To everyone else
who has read and encouraged me with this novel: Allegra
Moon, Carol Brock, Julie Incerti, Julie Hochfeld, Ann Boccino,
Ann Stigall, Barbara Davidson, Susan Thomas, Sally Underwood,
Jeannie Moglewer, and Cindy Forsyth, Ellen Montalbin, Chris,
Liz, and Marguerite Gole, Sue and Rene Chouteau, Jodie Ellis,
Deborah Hodeson, Liz, Danielle and Thomas Moulia, Cyrille
Patterson, and Seraina Conrad. To my amazing editor, Karen Li,
who has a real *Talent*. And to my golden loves Steve, Jessica,
and Michelle Davidson for lighting up my life with joy.

– *Ellen Dee Davidson*

STOLEN VOICES

written by
Ellen Dee Davidson

Lobster Press ™

Chapter 1

DEMONSTRATION DAY

"I WISH MIRI were here."

It's hard to resist the impulse to run over to my best friend, Jalene, to tell her that I wouldn't miss her Demonstration for the world. But instead, I hide deeper in the shadows of the trees closest to the outdoor stage and nervously twist my long, red braid between my fingers.

The crowd buzzes with anticipation at the first Demonstration of the spring season. Giggles of nervousness erupt from the stage wings where my friends are waiting, unseen by the audience. One of the few adults in a white gown puts her finger to her lips and shakes her head to signal quiet.

Jalene looks anxious and thrilled at the same time. No wonder. After the Masking, the Demonstration is the most important event in a fifteen-year-old's life! Having spent most of our time in training for the last five years, we reveal our deepest soul gift, our Talent, to the community on this day.

I shift to look at the crowd assembled before the stage. My parents, who sit up front with the other Important Officials, have different reactions to the excitement around them. Pater smiles indulgently at the noise and turns to say something to the young man sitting next to him. But Mater sits tense and upright, lips pursed. The Masker is everywhere in the crowd, shaking hands and smoothing down his long, black beard as he greets people with his hearty voice.

The elderly sit in the back rows. They look like pale butterflies in their shining pastel gowns. One very old woman rocks back and forth in her chair, actually chanting to herself. Sometimes the truly elderly do this when their Masks start to thin. No one worries about it too much; old peoples' voices are too worn and feeble to be a threat.

The Masker, resplendent in his gold gown, strides up to the microphone. "Welcome, welcome, to the spring Demonstration." His full voice rolls out in a glittery gilt wave, sending shivers up my spine; just listening to him always makes people feel good. All eyes fasten on the Masker. A palpable hush settles over the small crowd, and I let out a long, sad, but relieved sigh. No one will notice me now; not even my younger brother, Darin. At the moment, he is staring intently at the stage, just like the rest of the audience. I'm stabbed with a twinge of guilt for not telling him I was going to be here.

"I'm sure we are in for a treat this afternoon," booms the Masker. "This is a very successful group. They have all sorts of delightful and varied Talents to share with us before the Masking next week."

Talents that everyone else had to keep a secret. I can't keep back the bitter thought that the Masker obviously used a broad definition of a "successful group."

He unfurls a white scroll. "First, we will invite Eris to perform."

Eris bounces out onto the stage with a big grin on her face. She is never afraid of anything. She faces the crowd and smiles, taking a graceful bow before closing her eyes and then soaring high up in the air. She drifts over our heads, doing airy somersaults, dives, glides, and one long last swoop, buzzing low above the heads of the amazed crowd.

I remember when Eris first levitated. Our group watched her in awe. The Training Instructor let us have half a day off because he was so delighted. He said that we were the first group in ten years to have a flyer.

Maybe I can fly, too. I close my eyes, looking inward, visualizing myself growing lighter and lighter, until I float up, up above the trees like Eris. The wind caresses my face and makes the leaves rustle. I can almost feel my long, lanky body gliding lazily across the blue sky, as carefree as a cloud. The crowd's praise washes over me.

"Next, we will have Ceiron," calls the Masker, jerking me back to reality.

Ceiron strides confidently to the front of the stage. And then he just stands there. He stands there with his ear cocked to one side. He stands there and looks out around the crowd. People shift nervously in their seats.

At last Ceiron bows. "Thank you. I've heard enough for today." I can almost hear the collective sigh of relief as he leaves the platform. No one is really comfortable with a listener. They hear too much—maybe even one's most hidden thoughts and fears. Fortunately, Ceiron is always polite about his ability.

I concentrate hard, trying to *hear* Jalene. I'd love to share my best friend's happiness over showing off her Talent. But I don't catch even the whisper of a thought before the Masker introduces Nonce.

I cross my fingers for Nonce. She has a tendency to faint when she's too stressed or excited. But today she seems fine. She tilts her delicate, fair pixie face up to the sky and whistles. A blue jay flies down and perches on her outstretched palm.

Then she clicks her tongue and a squirrel darts out from his tree and chatters to her. Songbirds flutter around Nonce's face, and a fox even appears on the edge of the clearing. One elderly person cries out, scared at this unusual wild animal sighting. There aren't any large animals inside our Walled City, but the park does border one of the busiest entrances to Noveskina. The fox might have slipped in as farmers came through. Animals seem to do the impossible when they hear Nonce call.

The whole audience stands in appreciation. The people rub their hands together softly. Even I can't help myself. Nonce chirps and clicks goodbye to the creatures that encircle her like a living, breathing halo. They disperse, and she shyly leaves the stage.

The Masker returns to his scroll, then smiles. "Now we have Aron." My heart skips a beat as I lean forward for a better look.

Aron springs onto the stage, does a double back flip, two cartwheels, a walking handstand, and then a jubilant twirling leap. He stops for a second, flashing an exuberant grin and running his fingers through his tousled blond hair, and then jumps into the air, somersaulting once before landing again. Bless the Masker, Aron is cute! The people stand and flap their gowns in appreciation. Everyone loves a tumbler. Our whole group was so proud when it became clear that gymnastics would be Aron's Talent.

Suddenly, loud and clear, my name rings out across the park. "And now, Miri."

I freeze. *I shouldn't be on that list!* I wipe the sweat from my forehead as my mind races blindly. Of course I really want to perform. I am dying to be in the Demonstration with my friends.

There is only one problem.

I don't have a Talent.

(hapter 2

NO TALENT

I RUN. BLOOD pounds in my ears and tears blur my vision as I sprint across the park.

Jalene's voice follows me. "Miri!"

I don't look back, but I can feel everyone staring. I run faster, gulping air, pressing my side with my fist where it aches, racing across the damp grass, past the greenhouse with its orange and lemon trees, onto the crumbling asphalt of the street. I swerve around the decayed vehicles, overgrown with plants, and jump over the narrow canal. Windows in abandoned buildings glare at me as I race toward my own secret refuge.

The year we were ten, our Training Instructor told us it was time to find our sanctuaries. We were all so excited. The place we found would be ours alone. It would be a place where each of us could go to discover our deepest soul gifts. The instructor said we could search anywhere inside the Wall that surrounds the sparsely populated city of Noveskina. Once we found the area that pulled us in and made us feel secure and inspired, the instructor would help each of us perform a ceremony to seal the spot. No one else would be drawn there—and, in fact, they would overlook it if they were in the area.

Halfway to my sanctuary, I slow down, too winded to run

any farther. *Besides, what would be the point?* I've spent every spare minute there these past six months, and it hasn't solved anything. Sighing, I turn back in the direction of my house.

I place my palm against the recognition lock, and the front door opens. "Miri home," intones the mechanical voice.

Home. Where I shouldn't be. Kicking off my sandals, I jog upstairs to my sleeping chamber and collapse onto my lounge, panting. If only I had a Talent—like Jalene! My stomach twists. I didn't even stay long enough to hear Jalene's story. But, *noise and damnation*, what do I care? I hurl my satin pillow at the floor. *At least Jalene has a Talent.*

Curling into a little ball, I look around the room. I haven't spent much time in it these past five years. Since I reached ten years of age, I've spent most of my waking hours at the training center with the rest of my age-mates. A chorus of Noveskinian songbirds chirps outside my window. Normally I love the way their singing makes the colors swirl against the plastic windowpanes, but right now it just makes me feel sick.

My thoughts whirl in a jumble. *Jalene will still be my friend, but I'll be her inferior. And Pater will be so disappointed.* I imagine him looking at me with his sad, blue eyes. And Mater. I can just see her reaction, her thin upper lip curling in disgust as if I were nothing more than a worm. *Worst of all, what about Aron? There's no way he'd be interested in an UnTalented.* I fidget with my stack of learning cubes but don't bother to activate them. They haven't helped me find my Talent yet, and there isn't much hope they'll do so now.

The recognition lock interrupts my misery. "Darin home."

Straining my ears, I try to hear if my younger brother has any friends with him. If one person opens the recognition lock, others can slip in right behind without being announced. But I don't hear anyone else. Darin and I are the only ones home. We don't have any other siblings in our family. We should, to help raise the population, but Mater had some sort of accident, and now she can't have any more children. She's never told me what happened. But, then again, she never tells me anything.

Jumping up to look in the mirror, I straighten my gown. My hair looks wild, the red locks having escaped my usual braid. But what does it matter? I wipe the tears from my wide brown eyes just in time. Darin's already at the door. Even though we are close, it still embarrasses me to have him catch me crying.

"Miri?" Darin walks into my room. "I told you it would be a mistake to go," he says in his new know-it-all tone. But there is a kind expression in his eyes. I know he is concerned. "You'll find your Talent."

"That's easy for you to say," I groan. "You're only thirteen, and your Talent has been glimmering for two years already." I turn and flop back down onto the lounge. "I don't know how you'll hide it from Mater and Pater until your Demonstration."

Darin shrugs. "You know they're always at work...and I spend most of my time at the training center now. I'm just careful not to order them around."

I snort. "Your command Talent's not that good. There's no way you could order around two Important Officials."

"That's what you think," replies Darin, in that same obnoxiously, superior voice. He points at me "Get up!"

Automatically, I stand. "Oh, stop it," I mutter, sitting right back down. "Boss me again, and I'll stick you in the crypt."

Darin laughs and sits next to me. I used to be able to scare him with stories of Noveskina's crypt, but he's too old for it now. The crypt is a marble room deep under the ground where they bury the most Important Officials when they die.

Supposedly, it locks automatically after someone enters it. The Training Instructor once explained that this lock was put in place to prevent the escape of potential grave robbers. I didn't like that idea one bit when our class went down there for a tour. It was dark. And stuffy. Like my room is feeling right now.

I push my palms into my eyes and groan, "If only I had a Talent to surprise them with! Everyone else in my group has one. I should have an *extra* special Talent, being the child of two leadership adults! And, instead, I have nothing."

Darin grows serious. "You know that everyone gets Talents in their own time," he says, trying to sound reassuring. But he just sounds worried. Almost as worried as I feel.

"Uri home," intones the recognition lock. Pater's heavy tread crosses the tile floor. I don't hear the lock's next announcement, but there is no mistaking Mater's distinctive limp.

"Miri?" calls Pater.

I don't want to talk to my parents. Not after today. Looking out the window, I search for a way to escape. But my room is on the second floor, and it is a long drop down to the old city road.

The quiet adult voices of my parents drift up from the sharing room below. I hear them perfectly through the enameled heating vent. "I have never been so embarrassed," says Mater, slapping her bad foot against the floor the way she does when she is very angry. "It was all I could do to stay in my seat until the Demonstration ended."

Pater clears his throat. "Perhaps Miri has an explanation...."

"She had better," hisses Mater, "after the way she shamed us before the entire community!"

They don't know! Guilt makes me itch as I remember how I begged the Training Instructor to let me tell them myself. He thought I'd told them weeks ago that I wouldn't be in the Demonstration. But I hadn't. As the days passed, I kept hoping that a Talent would surface. And then, last night, when I knew there was no choice but to tell them, my parents were so busy with last minute preparations for the performance that I didn't even see them. Admittedly, I was relieved not to see them. I was still hopeful that a Talent would appear, just in time.

I shove Darin toward the door. "You talk to them! Tell them I'm not home! Tell them I'm asleep! Tell them I'm sick!"

Darin compels me with his eyes that are as green as Mater's. "No. You have to talk to them, Miri."

He waits. I know he's right.

"*Miri!*" Mater calls.

"I'll go with you," says Darin. Then he adds, in the manner that people always want to obey, "Come."

I follow Darin slowly down the stairs. My feet feel weighted, and each step takes enormous effort. Darin opens the door to the sharing room. "She's here," he says. He follows me in, sitting next to me on the lounge.

Mater stands stiffly by the white solar heater. Her frizzy red hair is knotted in a tight bun and her emerald eyes stare sternly into mine. "What is wrong with you? Why did you run from the Demonstration like that?"

Perching nervously on the edge of the lounge, I open my mouth, but no words come out.

"Full of secrets, just like your mater," Pater teases, tweaking my ear. Mater grimaces. Like many adult Noveskinians, she disapproves of physical contact.

I know Pater is trying to cheer me up by making light of the situation—turning it into another little family oddity like

Mater's mysterious limp. He doesn't realize it yet, but this is much worse.

"I *demand* an explanation." There is no lightness in Mater's tone.

"I—" I don't know what to say.

Darin gives me a questioning look.

I cannot bring myself to confess, and Darin knows it. I nod slightly, giving him permission to help me out.

"She doesn't have a Talent."

I stop breathing.

The silence is loud.

Pater's wail pierces the air. "Our child! Miri! An *UnTalented?*"

Mater looks at him, shocked. "Uri, your voice!"

Pater's voice really is strange—so full of emotion. I've never heard an adult sound like that. I'm appalled and embarrassed for him. But then I feel guilty because his feelings are for me. He pulls himself together. "I'm sorry," he apologizes. "I just...I can't believe this is happening to us."

Mater lifts her chin and stands straight and tall. "I had high hopes for Miri. But we will have to deal with the situation as it is. Of course," she adds calmly, "if Miri is Masked before she finds a Talent, she will never develop one."

My mouth goes dry. Mater has just stated my worst fear.

Pater puts a protective arm around my shoulders. "You could talk to the Masker," Pater says desperately. "You could ask him to give Miri an extra year to find her Talent."

"And if she doesn't find one?" Mater smoothes down her frizzy hair. "Talent or no Talent, Miri needs to be Masked and bonded with her age-mates. You know what happens otherwise."

Pater blanches.

I can't stand their bickering. "I want—"

"Be *quiet*, Miri." Mater's eyes narrow. "Can't you see we're having a crucial discussion?"

About me, and I'm not even allowed to speak.

Darin rolls his eyes sympathetically.

"Even if she doesn't find a Talent within a year, I'm sure the Masker could bond her with next year's class," Pater suggests, lightly squeezing my shoulder. "Then...it...wouldn't happen."

"That's highly irregular," says Mater, appraising me with a sweeping glance. "But, perhaps Miri does need more time. I'd like to see her become a first class citizen."

I wince. Although people rarely talk about it in polite society, I know that people in Noveskina aren't really all equal. A few oddballs are second class citizens— Masked and bonded, but unTalented. They end up doing lower status jobs, like arranging chairs at Demonstrations and delivering cubes. But they are, at least, more free than the third and bottom class, the house servants.

Pater's blue eyes widen with determination. "At least we'd know we've given her every chance. Talk to the Masker! He'll listen to you. He needs you for his work."

"You have the oddest ideas," Mater snaps. "Still, the Masker might do it for me." She sounds so smug that I feel a twinge of annoyance. Still, I realize what an honor it is that Mater can see the Masker at almost any time. Most people only see him in his official capacity, hosting Demonstrations and other events. An individual meeting with him is rare, indeed.

"Thank you, Uta! Thank you!" says Pater, shaking me like a rag doll.

Mater throws him a disgusted look. "You sound just like a child."

Pater tones his voice down to the careful neutrality

acceptable for adults. "I still think it's the right thing to do. After all, we are such a Talented family; Miri *must* have a Talent. We will wait."

"But I don't want to wait!" I moan. "If I'm not bonded with my age-mates, I'll lose all my friends!"

Pater gives me a comforting pat on my shoulder. "Yes," he says. "You will."

Chapter 3

THE SANCTUARY

AFTER A NIGHT of tossing and worrying, my whole body aches. The house servant taps on the door, and I force my eyes open. Nobody is around, so I try asking him a personal question. "How are you?"

The servant hands me my regular cup of broth without replying. I think it's stupid the way servants are never supposed to speak until spoken to, so I always try to get them to converse when no one is listening. After all, they must have *something* to say. But I understand that their voices are so weakened by their Masks that it sometimes hurts them to talk.

Gulping the clear liquid, I watch as he pulls up the thick drapes. The day is gorgeous again—cloudless and blue. If only I felt the way the day looked—full of promise and joy....

But a fog of grief spreads across my chest. After the house servant leaves, I reluctantly get up and slip a white training gown over my blue bodysuit. Then I open my sleeping chamber door and start down the stairs. The house is quiet. My shoulders relax. Mater and Pater are probably already at work, so I won't have to face them. They often go in on Sundays.

I tense as soon as I enter the eating room. Mater and Pater are right there, seated around the low table. Their faces look grim. Gulping, I take my seat. They don't say a word.

If only Darin were here. He's always good at relieving a tense situation. But he is probably at his command lesson or with his friends in the park. Sometimes I can't help wishing he didn't have a Talent yet—we used to spend a lot of time together with our parents working so much. But now, Darin is almost as busy as Mater and Pater.

The house servant walks in and sets a platter of smoked fruit, pickled fish, curdled pudding, and flat bread in front of us. We remain silent. There is only the faint scrape of wooden spoons on plastic bowls as he leaves.

Mater raises her slender hands over the food for the invocation. "We thank the earth for this food. We thank the Masker for the one song, one story, One Voice that gives us unity."

"We give thanks," Pater intones automatically, but I notice he doesn't sound very thankful. As for me, I can't even croak out the familiar words. My stomach churns.

I watch them eat. They pointedly do not watch me as I sit at the table, unable to touch my food.

Mater finishes her flat bread, wipes her mouth with a sea sponge, and then speaks to me for the first time this morning. "Pater and I are going to speak to the Masker. We are going to untangle the mess you've gotten us into."

I clench my hands. *How can she think it is my fault?*

"Stay here, and don't get into any more trouble," she adds, standing up.

Biting my lip, I force myself not to argue even though she is treating me like a child. It will only make her angrier. Instead, I watch numbly as Pater gives me a sympathetic smile before turning and following her out the door. My hopes go with them as their footsteps recede into the distance. They don't care what I want at all. They've already made up their minds to delay my Masking.

I'm so lost in my thoughts that I don't even hear the click of the recognition lock until it announces, "Jalene here." The door opens because Jalene, like all of our close friends, has been imprinted for our lock.

Jalene bolts into the room. "Miri, what happened?" she asks, brushing a black curl off her cheek and sitting on the cushion next to me. "Why did the Masker call your name?" Her dark eyes look troubled.

I shrug. "I have no idea, but he shouldn't have. I wasn't supposed to be on that list."

Jalene nods, but she has no idea how it feels to be humiliated in front of the whole community—and I am far too ashamed to tell her.

Jalene changes the subject, trying to cheer me up. "Did you see Aron? Wasn't he great?"

"Amazing," I agree, hoping she doesn't hear the quiver in my voice. "I wish he'd notice me," I say, trying to fake one of our usual conversations.

"I think he does," Jalene says loyally. "Haven't you seen the way he does his most difficult flips when you're around?"

I force a smile. Only yesterday her comment would have made me happy. Now it seems trivial. "I wish I'd seen your Demonstration. How did it go?"

Her face lights up. "Everyone said they loved it. I'll do some storytelling for you later."

I try to look happy, but I can't keep it up anymore. My head droops. "You're so lucky to have a Talent."

"Oh, Miri," says Jalene, "you *have* to have one." She chews her thumbnail and adds softly, "We're fifteen now. Everyone in our age group has a Talent."

"Except me." I wipe the hot tears out of my eyes before they have a chance to fall. Jalene doesn't know the half of it.

"I can't believe going to your sanctuary to find your soul gift didn't work."

"You know that I've gone there hundreds of times—nearly every day this year."

Jalene's brow puckers in a peculiar little frown, as if she is trying to decide something. Then she takes my arm. "Come on. I have an idea."

I don't budge. "It's no use."

Jalene yanks me up.

"I'm not supposed to leave the house."

"You have to," says Jalene, pulling me toward the door. "I have an idea. It might help you find your Talent."

For a second, I continue to resist her tug. Mater will be furious if she finds out I've disobeyed. But if Jalene does have a way to find my Talent, it will solve all my problems. I push my plate aside. Mater doesn't know what it's like to be me. I don't think she even cares.

We race past the usual dilapidated buildings found everywhere in Noveskina. They are interspersed with inhabited dwellings, many of which are decorated with gardens and plastic fences.

"Where are we going?" I ask, panting.

"You'll see," says Jalene, continuing to run.

Colorful gowns blur as I hurry by. Because it is a nice day, many adults are quietly practicing their Talents outside. Some adults fly overhead in city surveillance. Others are busy healing people with their hands or training the birds many Noveskinians keep for pets. I notice one man crafting all sizes of learning cubes out of the soft plastic salvaged from the dumps left from the old days. Another grown-up is in a white gown like ours, which means she's been Masked and bonded with her age-mates but without a Talent. She looks like the one who delivers our communication cubes. I asked my parents what her name was once, but they weren't sure if it was Blanne or Blanche.

We dodge around a large metal object—one of the transportation vehicles people used before the wars. They are rusted and abandoned all over Noveskina. People would like to see them cleared away—but with our small population and lack of heavy equipment, no one has the time.

A child is playing inside one of the vehicles. Jalene and I slow down, amazed by the sound we hear. She is warbling a tune—like the birds!

Two adults hurry over. "Hush!" chides the woman, obviously disturbed. "You know it's forbidden to make those sounds."

"It won't be too soon when this one is Masked," says the man.

The child quiets down, and Jalene and I continue our dash through the city. My legs are tired and rubbery by the time Jalene stops running. She turns and faces me with a serious look on her face. "Do you promise never to tell anyone where my sanctuary is?"

Chapter 4

THE MYSTERIOUS SERVANT

I GASP. "YOU'RE going to share your sanctuary with me?"

Jalene nods. "Everything becomes clear there. I just *know* you'll find your Talent. But you have to promise."

"Oh, Jalene, I swear!" I cry, overwhelmed by her generosity. "But how will you get me in? I thought the Training Instructor sealed each of our spots."

"I'll bet you can get in if you just stick close to me," answers Jalene. "Don't let go." She takes my hand and leads me across the bridge over a small canal.

We walk down an overgrown lane, around a bend, and start up a steep hill. A smudge of greasy, black smoke mars the clear sky. I guess by the telltale odor of burning that the plastic smelts are below. We are in the old, industrial section of the city. Scrap metal clanks coldly as servants throw junk into piles. I shiver and draw closer to Jalene.

"Isn't it dangerous for you to show me your spot?" I ask. "Remember that story about the man who stumbled into his wife's sanctuary, and their Talents got all mixed up?"

"I'll take the risk," Jalene replies, her fingers tightly gripping my own. "Ready?"

I nod.

We pass through a strange shimmer in the air, like a heat

mirage. My body meets resistance—I feel like I'm walking through water and have the urge to turn away. Jalene tugs my hand sharply, pulling me through the thick, warm air. Gasping for breath, I let her guide me a few feet further up the hill. We stop right below an obscure section of the Wall that I, of course, have never seen before. "Here it is," announces Jalene.

Craning my neck to look up, I can barely see the top of the huge stone edifice that surrounds our city.

"No one ever comes here," says Jalene, sounding pleased.

"It's lovely." I sit in grass at the base of the Wall, enjoying the warmth and the view of the red tile roofs of Noveskina mixed in with tall, spiking buildings left over from the old days. A brass bell hangs from the tallest spire, gleaming in the sun; it doesn't ring because the inner gong has been removed.

"Thank you so much for sharing this place with me," I say, realizing what a huge gift this is from Jalene. I have never shown *anyone* my spot.

She nods her head solemnly; for once the look in her eyes is dead serious. "I know you won't tell anybody."

"Never," I agree, feeling more hopeful. Maybe I *will* find my Talent here. "Do you think I should try breath meditation?"

"Sure," says Jalene. "I'll do it with you."

We concentrate on our breath, in and out, in and out, for a long time until a mantle of peace settles around my shoulders. I begin to slowly look inward, listening for the quiet sense of guidance our teacher taught us to find. Sorting through the conflicting feelings and emotions, I see my shame, like an ugly fog, clouding my mind. Below it is the fear that something is deeply wrong with me. With each breath, I let these thoughts and feelings go, digging deeper, looking for that core truth.

Listening to Jalene breathe along with me helps. I feel her knee next to mine, and the heat of the Wall warms my back. I keep breathing, seeking any trace of Talent. But there is only the dark emptiness; it stretches out as far as I can see, like a starless night or a deep pit. "It's no use," I say, surfacing at last. "I don't recognize any kind of Talent. There's just nothing unusual or special about me."

"Don't be silly," says Jalene. "Nearly everyone has a deep soul gift, except for the plastic miners and house servants, of course. They're a lower class. Yours must just be late in showing."

I think of the plastic miners in the old dumps, digging through the rubbish to find usable plastic. I'd hate a job like that. "You don't understand!" I cry, closing my eyes and covering my face. "If I don't find my Talent before the Masking ceremony, I won't be Masked with you! We won't be bonded. My parents are asking the Masker to give me an extra year to find a Talent."

Jalene gives a short, sharp gasp. She doesn't say anything for a while. Her eyes look huge and stricken. Finally, she speaks: "Have you ever thought of *pretending* you have a Talent?"

I snort. "Right. Everyone already knows I can't fly like Eris or talk with animals like Nonce. You know nobody listens to my stories the way they do yours. And how am I going to tumble like Aron when I can barely do a cartwheel?"

"There are other Talents," reminds Jalene. "What about massaging, inventing, or gardening? Have you tried them all?"

"Not gardening," I mumble. "But even if I do try it, the teacher will know in a second that mine is no true soul gift."

Jalene presses her fingers against her chin. "What about

faking that you're a listener, like Ceiron?" she asks. "He's so polite; he rarely shares what he hears."

"I'd hate to be a listener..." I say slowly. "They're so embarrassing to have around."

"You wouldn't *really* be a listener," muses Jalene, plucking an early daisy. "Besides, we all put up with Ceiron."

"That's what I mean. Even our group just 'puts up' with him." I dig my nails into the tough, grassy ground. "Still...if it's the only way...."

Jalene pats my hand. "You might be able to fool them long enough to get Masked with me."

I picture the sharp eyes of the Training Instructor and shake my head. "They'd test me to make sure. Especially since my Talent has been so late in developing." I shred a blade of grass into smaller and smaller pieces. "I'd hate to think what they'd do to me if they found out I was an impostor."

Jalene's eyes cloud over. "I guess it's too risky. But what are we going to do? Our friendship will be *ruined* if we aren't Masked together. We won't be bonded." She paces back and forth for a moment and then turns to me. "Maybe you will find your Talent in the 'one story.' I could tell it to you."

"It's worth a try," I say.

Jalene begins the "one story." She doesn't know the whole thing yet, but because storytelling is her Talent, she is being taught the history of Noveskina.

"In the beginning, there was chaos."

At first I don't listen. My thoughts run around in my head like rats, gnawing the inside of my brain. *I need a Talent. I need a Talent. I need a Talent*, now.

But Jalene's storytelling is powerful, and soon the edges of my anxiety dull as I begin to sense those times long ago.

When she describes the sun, I feel its burning heat. And when she tells of the crows, I hear their sharp, black cries. I can't help feeling a part of the scene, and I begin to sink into it. My spine roots into the earth, and my fingers tingle. Maybe this will work, I think, and I will recognize my Talent in the "one story."

"Neighbor fought neighbor, and city fought city. People bickered, argued, and raised their voices against one another. And since each person's voice was as strong as his enemy's, there could be no peace. But what followed was worse.

"An evil man came to power. He discovered a way to condense the clashing noises and use them for destruction. Armed with the forbidden instruments, he and his followers annihilated city after city. Thus began the sound wars that raged for decades."

Jalene's voice rises with passion. "In desperation, Noveskinians turned to the one man who offered a solution, the Masker. Using the Masks, he united their voices into the one song, One Voice. Working together, the people managed to build the sound Wall and save Noveskina from destruction."

Suddenly I hear a strange crooning, and a swirl of rosy color billows around me. "What's that sound? Where did those colors come from?"

"I heard the sound," says Jalene. "But what colors?"

A mechanical voice interrupts. "House servant here."

"I didn't know there was a recognition door in this part of the Wall!" exclaims Jalene.

The smooth gray wall splits, giving us a brief glimpse of lush greenery. Close to the ground, a pair of topaz eyes winks out from the tangled vines. And then someone appears.

For an instant, she looks gowned in silver, just like my parents and the other Important Officials. But the gown dims to the white apron of a typical house servant. She walks through, carrying a large basket of produce, pausing when she sees us. For a long minute, she looks down at us with her level, gray eyes. "Good afternoon."

Jalene's jaw drops open.

The servant quickly bows her head and bustles down the road.

"The nerve!" says Jalene. "Can you imagine that? She actually spoke to us!"

I jump up to watch the servant go. Then I pace across the grassy hilltop. It doesn't make sense. I had barely been able to enter Jalene's sanctuary with her there, guiding me. How had this mere servant managed to walk right through the protective seal? And worse, would she tell her master that she'd seen me here? Turning to Jalene, I blurt, "Who is she? Where is she assigned?"

Jalene just continues to stare at the Wall, obviously as mystified as I am.

"And why did her gown change color like that?" I press.

Without taking her eyes off the Wall, Jalene murmurs, "I don't know." There is no hint of the recognition door anymore, only unbroken stone. She frowns. "I've spent more days than I can count here, and no one has ever come through before."

"How come she didn't use the main door over by the park?" I ask, looking around anxiously.

Jalene doesn't answer. She rubs her hand against the Wall, feeling for a crack.

I can't stop pacing. "Have you ever seen what's on the

other side of the Wall?"

"Only this glimpse just now," answers Jalene. "But I've always been told that, aside from the reclaimed farmlands, there's only the rocky seacoast to the west and the deadlands in every other direction."

"But I saw greenery!"

Jalene tugs at her curly hair. "Did you see those eyes peering out from the greenery? What *was* that?"

"I don't know," I answer, "But I've heard rumors that there are more wild animals out there than there used to be. Remember that fox that came to Nonce at the Demonstration?"

Jalene shudders. "That's why I'm happy we have the Wall. Some of those wild animals might be dangerous."

I nod. "Let's get out of here."

Jalene starts walking down the steep hill. "Where do you think the house servant came from?"

"She could have come from the farmlands," I answer slowly. "She had that produce...."

Jalene shakes her head. "She wouldn't have used this door. Farmers always use the park door. And this is as far from the farms as you can get. Do you think she could be from the Secret Valley?" she asks suspiciously.

"There's no such thing as the Secret Valley," I laugh. "That's just an old children's story. You, of all people, should know that everything outside the Wall was destroyed by the sound wars."

Jalene bobs her head in agreement, and I follow her down the narrow lane between the overgrown shrubs. "I wish I knew who that servant was though," she says, pushing a prickly branch out of her way. "I'd like to tell her master about her rude behavior."

We come out of the lane, onto a small knoll, and I can see the large, white building of the training center looming in the center of town. Suddenly, solving the mystery of this servant doesn't seem very important. "I don't care about her," I whisper. "The only thing I care about is finding my Talent."

Chapter 5

SOUND PRINTING

BY NEXT MORNING, neither Mater nor Pater has mentioned my Masking. No one has barred me from attending purification week. And no one stops me when I open the training center door.

Like many things in Noveskina, the doors are a multi-colored mash-up of recycled plastics. They open into the large, bare room that is the elite training center of Noveskina. Jalene hurries over to me. "Did you make it home before your parents?"

"Barely. They came home for the mid-day meal. We arrived at almost the same instant, so I pretended I was sitting on the front steps waiting for them."

"Close!" exhales Jalene. "Your mater is so strict. Remember the time with the lip coloring?"

I laugh. When Jalene and I were eight, we decided to use Mater's lip colors while playing dress up. Even though Mater never raised her voice once, she seemed mad enough to kill when she found us covered in the stuff.

"I think she was more upset about how loud we were laughing than about the fact that we'd used a whole stick of her purple gloss! Anyway," I add, sighing, "she didn't stop me from coming to purification week. Maybe the Masker refused to delay my Masking." I smile feebly. "At least I'll be bonded with you."

"Thank the Masker," says Jalene solemnly, taking my hand and pulling me to the front of the sparsely furnished room. "I couldn't stand it if anything came between us. But wouldn't your parents have told you if he refused their request?"

I shrug as we sit on the carpet. "I hardly ever see them. Most of our communication is by cube." I fiddle with the end of my braid, breaking off several split ends. Then I look up, staring into Jalene's eyes. "The worst thing would be not to be bonded with you and our friends. But I don't want to be Masked without a Talent! You have to help me find one before it's too late!"

The Training Instructor strides to the front of the room, cutting off conversation. Our instructor is a humorless man with droopy, wide, gray eyes and thick, fleshy lips. His muddy-green gown stretches tightly over his belly, and he loves the sound of his own voice. He used to like me. He must have figured that, as the daughter of two highly Talented Important Officials, I would be one of his most promising students. And, of course, he loves to take credit for his students' accomplishments. Unfortunately I don't have any.

Clapping his hands for our attention, the instructor says, "Today is a significant day."

With so much to worry about, I can tell it will be hard to focus on his usual long-winded speeches. I drop my head into my hands and sigh.

Jalene squeezes my hand and whispers, "Don't worry. I'll help you."

The Training Instructor pauses. His voice is as unvarying as that of most adults, but his eyes glare at Jalene. He hates it when anyone talks during his lessons. "As I was *saying*," he continues, "for the beginning of this week, you will sound print your gowns with symbols of your Talent." He points to a stack of satiny white material. "This fabric is specially treated to interact with your voice. There are no two voices alike, just as there are no two Talents exactly alike. In fact, as you should know by now, your Talent is reflected in your voice. It is what makes your voice—and you—unique."

The instructor stops and looks around the room, his eyes flickering past me as if I'm not even here. He resumes his speech, but my ears are buzzing with embarrassment. His meaning is clear. *If I don't have a Talent, I am not unique.*

"Wear it long enough, the special fabric will eventually react to the sound of your voice and print on its own. The science behind this material is known only to the Masker and select Important Officials."

I stare curiously at white robes and wonder if Mater is one of the "select Important Officials."

"However," the instructor drones on, "once you are Masked, your voices will lose the strength to print. Therefore, we have to amplify your imprinting ability before you are Masked. Years ago, a woman with inventing Talent came up with an idea to help us do this."

The Training Instructor holds up a funny-looking device. "This sound printing machine will speed up the impigmentation process. It will recognize and make a print for any known Talent."

The machine has a small mouthpiece attached to a tube with what looks to be a suction cup at the end. "I know this will be difficult. It goes against everything you've been taught," says the Training Instructor. "But for once, I'm going to ask you to make the forbidden sounds. To *sing*."

Everyone stares at him, wide-eyed.

"No one will be able to hear you," adds the instructor

hastily. "You will sing into this mouthpiece. When the machine registers your true note—the voice of your Talent—your gown will begin to impigment. This is a lengthy process as you must make a sound for every square inch of fabric."

The Training Instructor passes out the sound printers. "Before we begin, there are two more things. Keep your attention on your own gown and not that of your neighbors. That means no roaming eyes! And there is to be absolutely no talking. Not one word. Any sounds, other than the ones I make speaking through this sound diffuser," he holds up a plastic machine with a small end to speak into and a large, flat end pricked with holes, "will distort the impigmentation. Then your Talents will not be correctly recorded on your gowns." His heavy lips curl in a half smile. "In other words, I can talk but you may not!"

Nudging Jalene with my elbow, I give her a worried frown.

Jalene mouths, "Mid-meal."

I nod. We'll figure something out then. We have to.

The teacher hands the gowns out to all nineteen of my age-mates. He gives the last gown to Aron and then looks around, gazing intently at each one of us.

I rub the white material between my thumb and forefinger. It is silky and strong, made to last a lifetime. Then I pick up the sound machine. *Maybe* it *will discover my Talent.* Placing my mouth around the tube, I make my voice hum. The sound feels strange and forced in my throat, but the machine immediately collects it all. Not a note escapes into the room. I check the material of the gown attached to the suction cup. It hasn't changed.

I peek at Jalene to see if her gown is changing.

"Miri, please keep your eyes on your own work." The

instructor's voice wavers eerily through his sound diffuser.

Moving the cup, I attach it to a sleeve. This time, I take a breath and make my voice as strong and as deep as I can.

The cloth doesn't change.

I roll my eyes to the side, trying to see Eris's gown. Is that a hint of blue?

Determined, I sing harder. It won't be long now before I've printed every square inch of cloth. My voice is growing hoarse from the effort. Obviously, singing is nothing to be missed. I straighten my head and take the tube out of my mouth, swallowing around the lump in my sore throat.

Aron glances at me sympathetically. Sound printing is probably too sedentary for him. He's much happier jumping around. He lets go of his sound machine long enough to hold his neck in a mock choking gesture.

I grin, and my heart fills with a sunny glow. Maybe Jalene is right and he does like me. Maybe it won't matter to him if I never find a Talent. At least we'll still be Masked and bonded.

Happily, I sing into the machine. My mind is so occupied that it doesn't seem long before I have sound printed the last bit of fabric. Looking up, I notice all my friends are still hard at work.

Jalene's gown has turned a gorgeous shade of purple. It must be her Talent color.

Ceiron's gown is now a buttery yellow and depicts a crowd of people. One person stands off to the side.

Aron's blazing orange gown has tumblers doing handsprings across the hem.

"Miri!" admonishes the instructor through his diffuser. *"If I have to tell you one more time to keep your eyes on your own work, you will finish by yourself, outside!"*

I don't tell him I've already finished. Instead I look back

down at my gown, feeling sick. My gown hasn't changed at all. It is plain white—nothing like the gowns of my age-mates. It doesn't say a thing about me or my Talent because there is absolutely nothing to say. And this is how things are going to be from now on—Masked without a Talent.

Something needs to be done. Fast. I scribble on my cube and pass it to Jalene.

She bends down to read.

"What have we here?" asks the instructor, holding his hand out for the cube. He looks at it briefly. *"Miri, I'm disappointed that you feel your thoughts to Jalene are so momentous that you must interrupt her sound printing."* He purses his thick lips. *"Since you feel this is so urgent, I'll share it with the group."*

My ears burn.

"Jalene," reads the teacher. *"Help! Have to find Talent or be second-class citizen. Think of something! Anything! Miri."*

The class is silent.

The instructor clears his throat. *"This self-centeredness is unacceptable in an adult Noveskinian, Miri. And how you think your classmate can help you find a Talent, when I, with my particular expertise, have failed these past two years, I do not know."*

Resentment wells up in me. *As if you care. All* you *care about is hearing yourself talk!*

Ceiron stifles a snort. I figure that he listened in on my thoughts and give him a sharp look.

The Training Instructor lectures on, *"As a true Noveskinian adult, you will be expected to accept your place in society without further voicing of inappropriate complaints."*

He looks around the room. *"We'll break for mid-meal,"* he orders. *"Absolutely no talking. I do not want you to waste your voices."* He erases the cube, sets it next to my robe, and walks by without even glancing at me.

Jalene's eyes fill with sympathy, and she walks beside me as we head to the long table where we eat. It is covered in special food—exotic fruits like peaches for joy, fried octopus tentacles to symbolize commitment, and some wheat grains to add stability to our lives.

The Training Instructor uncorks a bottle of green liquid. He pours a bit into each of our silver goblets. "This sea-vegetable drink will soothe your vocal chords." The liquid fizzes and bubbles. It smells tart and sweet at the same time.

He raises his goblet high. "To your Masking!"

Chapter 6

MASKING DAY

IT HAS BEEN only four days since we finished imprinting our gowns, but to me it feels like four years. For the past two days, we've been going through the purification baths and listening to the Training Instructor's lectures on the importance of adult responsibilities. Today, we were sent home to rest before the big ceremony.

At first, I tried to relax, reclining on my lounge. I needed some sleep. I've been so wound up lately that my brain feels like mush. But I couldn't sleep. I couldn't even read; it was impossible to concentrate. I just kept thinking of more crazy Talents to try. At one point, I went outside and attempted a bit of earthworm farming and even plant psychology. It didn't work.

Although I hate him for saying it, the Training Instructor is right. The only thing I can do now is accept the fact that I don't have a Talent and behave like a mature, adult Noveskinian.

I look at myself in the mirror. Today is the day. Our Masking is only an hour away. And, believe it or not, I don't even know if I'm in the ceremony. Mater and Pater haven't been around to ask.

Even so, I tell myself, it is better to be prepared. I tame the tangles out of my wild, red hair and plait it into a single, neat braid down my back. Then I look at the clothes hanging in my wardrobe. It's tempting to put on the brilliant orange silk bodysuit I received for my last name day. I eye it longingly but then push it aside when I think of how the color will shine through my plain, white gown. I sigh and reach for the darker and more discreet midnight blue.

Just as I finish wriggling my long torso into the thin, stretchy material, the clear, angular communication cube beeps, requesting all fifteen-year-olds to meet at the training center. I give a sigh of relief. I'm going to be Masked after all. You'd think Mater and Pater would have found the time to tell me themselves.

As I jog down the stairs, I see a stack of communication cubes on a silver tray by the entryway. One is flashing red. I give it a wary look; if it's from my parents, I don't even want to know what it says. Besides, I justify, there is no time to read it now. I hurry out the door.

"Hey, Miri!" Darin pokes his head out his upstairs window as I cross the street. "Good luck today." He winks and then speaks in a high falsetto, like a little kid: "I command you to remember everything that happens and report back to me!"

Darin makes me laugh. Lately he's been taking his command Talent so seriously, bossing everyone around in earnest. To be honest, I was getting a little sick of him. I'm relieved to see that he hasn't completely lost his sense of humor. I smile and wave back. "You know I always tell you everything."

It is so early in the morning that I meet only waste reclaimers and farmers with produce on the street. Chilly air whips against my face. Shivering, I look up at the windows hoping to see a friendly face, but the windows are closed and shuttered against the cold. The feeble sun hides behind a cloud, and everything looks as bland and colorless as my gown.

Pressing on against the biting wind, I wonder what the

Masking ceremony will be like. It's a highly secretive ritual—only the Masker and select Important Officials take part in the ceremony—and none of the adults I know seems to remember what happens. Of course, Mater would know, but she never tells me anything.

As soon as I walk into the center, I see my age-mates milling happily about the large room, looking beautiful in their new gowns, a rainbow of colors.

"Hey, Miri!" Eris floats over to me with her brilliant blue gown flapping around her like a set of wings. She laughs giddily. "I'm having a really hard time keeping myself on the ground today."

Aron taps his foot and snaps his fingers, obviously impatient to get moving. His flashing black eyes are so bright in contrast with his blond hair and poppy orange gown that I can't resist smiling at him.

He does not smile back.

I shift from one foot to the other, wishing I could think of something to say—something witty and brilliant. But the grin freezes on my face as his glance travels down to my white gown. He frowns and turns away from me.

My ears burn hot, and I imagine that they are bright red, too.

"Don't worry about him," whispers Jalene, coming up and putting her arm around me. "He just needs a little time to get used to it. Anyway, just think!" She sweeps her arm out to gesture at the huge, sparsely furnished room that echoes as she speaks. "This is our last day at the center. Finally, we're done with this place! And, after today, we'll be bonded."

"I'm glad my Masking wasn't delayed. I'm sure waiting a year wouldn't have done anything," I add. "I'd just end up bonded with a bunch of kids I don't even know. I'll have to make the most of what I have."

"Sure," agrees Jalene quickly, tossing her curls out of her eyes. "And you'll always be part of our group now, and we'll always be friends."

I scratch my arm and hope that she is right. "I forgot to tell you how gorgeous you look today," I say, changing the subject. Her gown really is pretty, with pictures of Noveskinian history parading across the deep purple.

Before Jalene can respond, an adult walks in. He is cloaked and hooded in the silver gown of leadership. It isn't until I hear his familiar droning voice that I recognize the Training Instructor. "Congratulations, students. After today you will be joined as never before and transformed into true parts of the adult community." The Training Instructor speaks slowly and ceremoniously. "Please line up and follow me to the ritual chamber," he continues, pointing to the arched metal door on the far side of the room. I look with surprise at the door he mentions. It's one we never use. One that has always been locked.

I cross my fingers. It looks like everything is going to work out after all. Jalene gets in line behind me. Ceiron stands in front. He turns to me, his startling violet eyes fixing on my white gown. "I'm glad you'll still be with us, Miri, even if you didn't find a Talent."

"Not having a Talent isn't that big of a deal." I try to sound casual, but my voice cracks. I know that all of my age-mates heard the Training Instructor read my cube to Jalene during the sound printing, so I can't pretend that the situation doesn't bother me.

Ceiron has a funny expression on his pale face. Suddenly, I wonder how Ceiron knew there was a chance I wouldn't be bonded with our group. No one but my parents, Darin, and

Jalene knew. And Jalene wouldn't have told. But—of course. The sour taste of disgust fills my mouth. Ceiron read my mind.

Ceiron says something, probably in answer to my thought, but his words get lost as the other students—nineteen in all—push behind him in their eagerness to get to the arched doorway.

The Training Instructor stands at the head of the line. There is another adult at the entrance, cloaked, hooded, and waiting. One by one, they admit the students. Eris is the first of my friends to go in. I watch the adult press something into her hand. It is hard to see beyond the doorway, but it looks like he's stamping her palm. Aron goes next. The instructor leads my age-mates into the pitch-black corridor.

Several students pass, and then it is my turn. I peer past the hooded adult and feel cold drafts. I can see by the instructor's lamp that the hallway is surprisingly wide. Two lines of columns stretch into the darkness. I look up at the adult. It is Pater.

His brows furrow. "What are you doing here, Miri? You must have received the urgent cube I sent you!"

Guilty, I stare at my feet.

"The Masker decided at the last second to grant you the extra year we requested," says Pater.

My heart hammers. "No! I don't want to wait!"

"Instructor!" calls Pater. "Take over for me for a minute. I have to make sure Miri leaves."

The Training Instructor's lips pucker in a frown. "What is the meaning of this? Miri is most certainly not leaving. It is her Masking day."

"She's not going to be Masked," says Pater. "She doesn't have a Talent."

"If she went through my program, she will be Masked with"

her age-mates, whether she has a Talent or not," the teacher replies.

"No one in my family is going to be Masked without a Talent!" snaps Pater with a childish rise of impatience in his voice. "We would have informed you earlier, but the Masker granted our request only an hour ago. Miri will have an extra year to find her Talent."

"I don't know what you did to pull this off," grumbles the Training Instructor. "You elites and your special privileges! I will not have any part of it. It is unfair and risky!" The instructor leans in toward Pater, dropping his voice down to a sharp whisper. "And what if she doesn't find a Talent in a year? She won't have the age-mate bond or a Talent, and you know what happens then...."

"She'll find a Talent," says Pater.

"Please, Pater. Let me be Masked with my friends," I beg.

"Don't argue with me, Miri," Pater says, pointing to the training room door. "Go home. Now!"

Pater's words, harsh as never before, slap me in the face. Too hot with fury to speak, I spin around. Jalene grabs my hand. "You can't go, Miri!"

I tug my hand out of hers and run. What choice do I have? Pater will never let me in.

I slam the plastic training room door behind me, not caring if it is an immature display of my feelings. Gulping in the fresh outside air, I try to calm my jangled nerves. But I can't. Pater's sharp tones ring through my ears. I thought he was different, but I can now see that he's no better than Mater. On a whim, I spin around on my heel and grab the door handle. *What do adults matter? I'm going to see the Masking of my friends!*

Carefully opening the door a crack, I glance furtively

around the training room. Everyone has gone through the arched doorway, leaving the main room deserted.

I tiptoe through the empty space and peek into the darkness of the wide corridor. Nonce is lying on the floor in a pool of light to one side. Pater is hunched over her, gently patting her face and trying to bring her back to consciousness. Poor Nonce. I imagine that she fainted as she often does when she gets too wound up.

Quickly, I take off my gown, wad it into a ball, and hold it under my arm; the white material would attract too much notice. Wearing only my midnight blue body suit, I take my chance.

It is surprisingly easy to slip into the corridor and past Nonce and Pater. I find the rest of my age-mates lined up along the right side of the hallway, waiting. I hide in the shadows behind a large column. Eventually, Pater leads Nonce over to the group and lifts a tubular object.

"Wait!" cries Nonce, springing back to full consciousness. "I don't like needles!"

Pater thrusts a quick jab into Nonce's palm. Immediately, she becomes calm. Her eyes don't even flicker when she sees me, but I press my index finger against my lips, begging for secrecy, just in case.

Everyone begins walking slowly down the gloomy, stone hallway. The glowing globes are the only lights we have. The instructor leads. Pater brings up the rear. Keeping to the center of the line, I dodge between the shadows of the columns and try to stay out of sight.

I shiver from the cold drafts but am secretly thrilled. I've never, ever, heard of anyone sneaking into a Masking ritual before. It's insane to try this. *What will they do if they catch me?* Pater is already mad at me. He'll be furious if he finds me here....

Sudden panic makes me stop. I decide to turn back before I go too far. Groping my way along the damp wall, I walk against the flow of traffic.

I see Aron drag along, strangely still. Jalene passes with a somber, plodding gait, but she doesn't see me. A flicker of light catches Ceiron's face, and I notice a dull, heavy-lidded expression in his normally watchful eyes.

At least it is easy to get past them. The gown bundled in my arms gleams in the dusky light. I know I should shove it in the deep pools of darkness behind the columns before it gives me away, but instead I clutch it tighter, hoping that Pater won't see it when I pass him. Trying to sound print this gown could be the last thing I'll have ever done with my friends.

Suddenly, a loud clang rings through the hallway. The metal door to the corridor has slammed shut. And, without a recognition pass, I'm stuck.

Pater's gown swish-swishes against the tile floor as he approaches, carrying the pale globe light. Darting back into the middle of the line, away from the lights, I pray to the Masker that Pater won't see me. My heart pounds so loudly that I am afraid the others will hear its echo off the old stone walls. I am the only one here who does not belong.

My bare feet slip against the smooth floor as we descend down and down. The globes cast eerie shadows. Cool, dank air rises, enfolding my body and giving me goose bumps. At last, we file into an oval room. Four marble pillars stretch up to the rounded ceiling, attaching with elaborate, carved moldings. Darting behind one of the pillars, I crane my neck toward the light to see what will happen next.

"Welcome to the ritual chamber," says the Training Instructor. There are sumptuous satin pillows strewn about the thickly carpeted floor and lavish tapestries hanging from the stone walls. It is even warm, I realize gratefully.

"This is the 'egg' room from which you will be newly hatched," continues our former teacher. My friends are so quiet that I can't even hear them breathe. "First, the Masker has a few words for you."

A puff of smoke fills the air with the smell of incense. My eyes water from the smoke as I see the Masker shuffle forward with a limping step. The hairs on my arms stand. His posture is erect, almost rigid, but his beard is a scraggily snow white.

"He looks...older," Jalene mumbles groggily.

It's true. In training we learned that he has served Noveskina for generations. But I've never seen him look so ancient. I could swear that his beard was black at the Demonstration a week ago.

"Welcome to your transformation, students," says the Masker. His voice is different from his usual gleaming copper tones. It sounds worn and gravelly—a dingy, gray sound. He motions to another adult waiting in the wings. Shuffle, step, shuffle, step. It is Mater! Her face glows with pride as she lifts a cloth to reveal a big vat. Pater and the Masker peer at what lies within. The Masker nods approval.

Mater reaches in and pulls something out. It is squirming, flesh-colored, and translucent. I lean in for a better look. The thing looks wet and sticky. Alive.

"A Mask!" I gasp.

The Masker's head shoots up.

Too late, I realize my mistake.

The Masker turns and stares straight at my corner of the room.

Chapter 7

THE BONDING

SHRINKING DOWN INTO the dark puddle of shadow behind the pillar, I keep perfectly still.

"Who said that?" the Masker says quietly. "Maybe they need another dose?"

"They all look relaxed to me," Mater answers smoothly. Her voice floats as if from a distance—detached.

There is a moment of silence. A long moment. Holding my breath, I peek around the column.

The Masker's gnarled, age-spotted hands are clenched in concentration. "I don't *hear* any stray thoughts," he says at last, but his body is still hunched over like a vulture.

A jolt of alarm shoots through me. *He is a listener?*

Instantly following my fear, the Masker glances around the room, searching, alert. I huddle deeper inside myself, finding that still, black place of quiet.

"We should begin before this Mask dries out," reminds Mater, handing the Masker a filmy, flesh-toned face.

The Masker straightens up, but his posture is still like an old man's—stiff and rigid. With one last glance around the room, he walks over to Jalene with the squirming Mask. "I give you this Mask so that the voice of your Talent will shape itself to the needs of our community and not be too strong for us to bear."

I risk poking my head a little further out from behind the marble column. Pater and the Training Instructor hold Jalene's head back; they grip her tightly, but she does not struggle. The Masker carefully spreads the wet flesh over Jalene's skin. For an instant, there is a sizzling sound and then a slightly scorched smell before the Mask grips onto her face and neck, sealing at her throat.

My stomach heaves. This isn't the beautiful rite of passage I expected.

A deep note rings, and brilliant purple, the same shade as Jalene's gown, flares out from her throat, circling up around her head and floating across the room. It casts an odd light, but otherwise, Jalene doesn't look any different than she did before.

One by one, the rest of my friends and age-mates are Masked. Each time, Mater shuffle-steps over to the large ceramic tub and selects another wriggling Mask out of the steamy vat. She then hands the translucent flesh to the Masker, who repeats the same words to each student: "I give you this Mask so that the voice of your Talent will shape itself to the needs of our community and will not be too strong for us to bear."

For every student Masked, a sound fills the room followed by a flare of color that erupts from the person's throat. Only they aren't all purple. Aron's is a vivid orange. His body stiffens, and he stands rigidly after the Mask is sealed.

As the Mask seals over Eris's voice box, there is a lovely hum and then a swirl of bright blue. She levitates a few inches off the floor. Then she drops back down with a dull thud, and the blue floats off, away from her body.

Pater grips Ceiron's head tightly, and my friend whimpers as the Training Instructor smoothes the Mask over his contorted features. Ceiron writhes as his flesh sizzles. There is a soft trill before a spurt of yellow pulses from his throat, and then his face goes deadpan.

As each student is Masked, colors fill the room, swirling and dancing, leaving only a few inches of clear space around the Masker. It almost makes me feel dizzy watching them. Perhaps it affects the other students too, because they shift their bodies and twitch.

"I think it's time," says Mater.

The Masker bows his head, his expression serene. All four adults raise their hands in what looks like an invocation and chant, "May you speak with the One Voice. May you be joined in unity."

The Masker places his palms on his temples and closes his eyes. He takes a deep breath and croaks out a feeble sound. His voice is as raspy as that of a house servant. He clears his throat and tries again. This time, the colors swirling around the room pause. For the third time, the Masker inhales deeply, shuddering, and forces his voice into a loud, hoarse chant. The colors freeze, hanging suspended in the air.

I cannot believe what I am seeing.

The Masker opens his mouth and drinks greedily. He sucks in each color, one at a time. Jalene's deep purple, Aron's bright orange, Nonce's woodland green. My friends lean forward, as if they are trying to follow their colors. Ceiron places his hands over his throat and winces, as if the Masker is somehow hurting him. The room grows blacker as the Masker inhales, even the lights seem to flicker, but he starts to glow.

I dig my nails into my palms.

The fatigue lines around the Masker's eyes disappear. His beard turns from white to black. Even his rigid posture becomes more natural as he sips in the last deep blue—Eris's color. He stretches luxuriously. "Ahh...that is better."

The rich yellow tones of his voice, now renewed, light up the room.

Slowly at first, and then gaining strength and power, the Masker begins to sing: "One song, one life, one verse...." It is unbelievable. It is nothing like the feeble warbling of the young children or elderly. His rich tones fill the room, fill my soul, and fill the empty spaces inside of me that I didn't even know existed until I find tears rolling down my cheeks.

My friends sit perfectly still, entranced. Their Masks sprout colored bands from the bases of their throats. The bands expand with the Masker's song; Jalene's purple touches and locks with Ceiron's yellow, and so on throughout the group. The bands grow until all the students have been connected by thin streams of colored light.

My heart clenches. The bonding.

The Masker's song deepens and swells until he sustains one, long bass note. Tingles shoot up my spine. I hold my breath as he projects the note in an almost golden stream. His voice wraps around the ribbons of light that connect my friends. It gathers them up, braiding them together into a single cord that leads directly to the Masker's own throat.

The song is over. My heart yearns for the sound. I ache for the Masker to continue.

"I think the bands are in place, Uta," he says.

"Yes," Mater agrees, her green eyes glowing with satisfaction. "Everything has gone well. Now they can be easily managed. It will save you much precious time and energy." She smiles at him. "Another group of Noveskinians will contribute to the oneness of our city."

The Masker smiles fondly at Mater. "I don't know what I'd

do without you, Uta." Even in the dim light, I can see that Mater is positively glowing from the compliment.

Once more, the Masker places his palms against his temples, closes his eyes, and inhales. When he opens his eyes, he chants a piercing, but incredibly sweet, high note. My age-mates start stretching and talking, acting more like the people I know.

"When are we going to be Masked?" asks Eris. Her voice sounds flat and empty.

"You are already Masked," says the Training Instructor, his puffy lips hinting at a smile.

Aron touches his face. His tone is dull. "I can't even feel it."

"The changes are subtle," explains the instructor. "You will notice them over the next few weeks."

"You are now bonded, too," says Mater.

Nonce touches her face softly with her long, tapered fingers and then looks around the circle at the others. "Why can't I see the bonds?"

Jalene's face is disappointed. "Yes, why can't we tell they are there?"

I stare at my friends, confused.

"I am the only one who can see the bonds," the Masker declares.

I don't understand. The bonds are perfectly obvious to me.

The Training Instructor claps his hands. "Enough questioning! It's time for the graduation feast."

Everyone lines up. They talk in their new, quiet adult voices as they file out of the room and start back down the long hall. I count them silently in my mind. All nineteen of my schoolmates have passed through the doorway with the three adults. I prepare to slip out behind them when someone suddenly clears his throat.

I freeze. The Masker is still in the room!

Chapter 8

CAUGHT

"WHO IS STILL here?"

I don't say a word, scarcely daring to breathe.

Although he limps, the Masker's tread is light and young as he strides toward my corner.

Looking around, I search frantically for a way to escape.

"How long have you been here?" asks the Masker gruffly, staring down at me.

Instinctively, I lie. "I just came...looking for my pater."

He speaks sharply. "How would you know your pater was here?"

"I—I saw him come in, with the others, before the Masking...."

"You must know you aren't allowed in the ritual chamber!"

I gulp. "I'm sorry." My heart flutters nervously as I give my feeble explanation. "But I had to speak to Pater."

The Masker gives me a searching look. "You must be Miri," he says thoughtfully. His manner becomes more courteous.

My heart hammers. "Yes."

"And you weren't here for the Masking."

I shake my head in an emphatic lie. "No. I just got here."

"You'll have to leave the back way with me," he says, extending his hand and pulling me up. My palms are moist with sweat, but the Masker's grip is firm—too firm to break.

Clutching my gown in my other hand, I stumble along beside him across the egg-shaped chamber. He takes me to the back of the room and moves an amethyst tapestry stitched with gleaming jade threads to one side, revealing a dark tunnel.

Once we walk into the tunnel, it becomes too dark to see, but the air has a curious pleasant scent. It is like something I've smelled before, although I can't quite place it. Roses? Bread? Sage? It is a combination of all of them mixed with the tang of lemon. I sniff appreciatively.

"You're right to pay attention to smell," the Masker says. "It's really the only way to navigate through these tunnels since they all look the same. In the old days, these tunnels were sewers; they used to smell terrible. But now we employ them as passageways for the servants and the occasional Important Official. I have the house servants scent them regularly so that we can find our way around without getting lost."

I am confused by the Masker's friendly tone. *Aren't I in trouble?*

We stop suddenly. The Masker puts his palm out and touches something.

"Masker here," recites the mechanical voice.

The tunnel wall opens, and we walk through into a sumptuous entryway. It is laid out like ours, only much fancier. I quickly note the mosaic tile floor, sculptures, and pure silver cube table. The Masker hangs his gown, nearly the same shade of gold as his voice, along with my white one. Then he leads me into the sharing room.

He sits down on the plump pillows and gestures for me to do the same. I perch nervously beside him and fiddle with the velvet edging of my cushion.

"It is understandable that you came to find your pater after receiving the urgent cube he sent to you," the Masker muses. "It must have been a shock for you to discover that you weren't to be bonded with your age-mates."

Too scared to speak, I give a small nod.

He looks stern. "Still, at your age, you should certainly know better than to come into the ritual room without an invitation. It's a good thing for you that the door is always locked. You couldn't have gotten in until after the initiation."

My stomach knots with anxiety. "I'm sorry. I didn't mean to."

"Well, never mind that," the Masker continues. "All's well that ends well. You had better head home now. I'm sure your mater will be worried about you. And," he wags an almost friendly finger at me, "no more sneaking around!"

I stand. "I won't do it again."

"No harm done." The Masker winks. "You'll have your Masking next year, after you've found your Talent."

I breathe a sigh of relief. I had no reason to be so frightened. The Masker has always been one of the warmest, friendliest adults in the community. *And now he looks and sounds like himself again—vibrant and young.*

The Masker suddenly stands and clenches my arm. "So you did see the ritual." His voice drops to a carefully controlled softness that is more terrifying than a yell. I cringe. I knew he was a listener! *How could I have let my thoughts slip?*

The Masker stares at me hard with his fathomless black eyes. "Your thoughts were not worth commenting on before— childish worries about getting in trouble. But now...."

Nervously, I look away, stammering. What excuse can I possibly make?

The door to the adjoining room opens. A slender servant wearing a bland, white apron walks through.

"Shut that door!" the Masker orders.

The servant closes the door, but not before I catch a glimpse of the strangest room. There is a large piece of furniture in one corner with black and white rectangles. It is vaguely familiar. My mind gropes, and then it comes to me—it must be a piano, like the ones we studied in the history learning cubes. One of the forbidden instruments.

The Masker turns his gaze back on me. Then he smiles, a chilling smile that makes me shiver. "I guess it doesn't matter that you've seen my instrument room after all." He pulls me after him. "Come on in. I'll show you the rest."

The dark-haired servant seems to be making an odd little sound under her breath as we pass her, but I don't have time to figure out if she is trying to say something. She stays in the sharing room as the Masker leads me into the unfamiliar instrument room and shuts the door behind us.

"That is a bassoon," the Masker says almost fondly, pointing at a strange, shiny brass instrument. "Over there is my collection of drums and a cello, and this is a trumpet."

I shift nervously from foot to foot. *Why is he showing me all of this?*

The Masker chuckles to himself, picks up the trumpet, and blows a loud note. I jump involuntarily. The note is harsh and loud. It leaves an ugly smear of brown dangling in the air.

The Masker gives a satisfied nod. "These instruments are very powerful. Too powerful. Played, they can change the way people feel—make them happy, sad, excited, afraid."

I silently agree. It scared me half to death.

"I should have destroyed them all to prevent them from ever being used to fight another war." He sighs. "But I couldn't resist keeping a small collection." He gives me a friendly look.

Maybe he isn't going to do anything to me.

The Masker answers my thought. "Don't worry, Miri. You're going to be fine." Some of the tension melts out of my body, and I look around, trying to commit all the details to memory so that I can tell Darin and Jalene. They'd both be fascinated. Darin always wants to know about everything. He says that you can't command people without some understanding of how things work.

"Some of these instruments are impossible to manufacture these days. Many resources were destroyed in the wars. We've lost the machinery that makes things like this," he says, waving the trumpet. "And the only metal we have is that from salvaged vehicles and dumps. Still," he says, fondly stroking the lustrous dark wood of the piano, "it would be possible to copy some of the simpler instruments if it weren't so dangerous. They could fall into the wrong hands. But, fortunately, these are the only instruments left and nobody knows about them."

Then why is he telling me?

Once again, he answers my thought. "Oh, it doesn't matter if I tell you now. You will stay here until you are Masked. Once you are Masked, I won't have to worry about you saying anything I don't wish you to say."

"It's too late to Mask me with my age-mates," I protest. "And the next group won't be ready for a year."

"That is a shame," he agrees affably. "But it cannot be helped. I wanted to give you time to find your Talent. Your mother and I had such high hopes.... But we had trouble with you. Perhaps you wouldn't have developed one anyway."

"What trouble?"

"When your mother was pregnant," he replies. His fingers ripple absently over the piano keys, making a beautiful sound that doesn't ease my fear at all. "You needn't concern yourself," he adds, forestalling the questions I am dying to ask. "I just wish you had a Talent, or that I'd been able to Mask you with your age-mates." He shrugs. "But you've seen too much to go freely in Noveskina without a Mask. I just don't know how I'll explain it to your mother."

"Explain what?"

The Masker closes a lid over the piano keys. "Without an age-mate bond or a Talent, you will have to be Masked immediately—as a house servant."

Chapter 9

SONGBIRDS

I STARE AT the Masker, disbelieving. "You can't mean that!"

"I never say anything I don't mean," answers the Masker smoothly. "Come." He motions for me to follow him.

My knees are so wobbly that it is hard to walk. How can he want to Mask me as a lowly house servant? No one in our elite class ever becomes a house servant. New servants are always either the children of servants, or scavengers brought in from the deadlands. Those in our class without Talents are still bonded, still socially accepted, even if they do the less exciting jobs.

It is too horrid. House servants have practically no voices at all.

The Masker unlocks a heavy door. "Watch your step," he cautions courteously.

Following him down the stairs, I want to shout, cry, kick, scream, and yank his awful beard, but I know that won't get me anywhere. A thin thread of steely resolve tightens my shoulders. I can't let myself think about this right now. If I do, he will hear me. Breathing deeply, I quiet my mind, hoping that he hasn't already heard too much.

The twilight air is damp against my face as I walk down the steep terra-cotta stairs. My throat feels thick and closed, but I clear it and ask, "Where are we going?"

"I want to show you something," says the Masker, walking briskly, his right foot dragging quickly behind him. Soon we find ourselves in front of a latticed net door. He parts it and holds it open for me to walk into what looks like a learning cube picture of a lush jungle. Fronds of green with gorgeous blooms and tall trees reaching high fill the area. Best of all is the delightful medley of hundreds of chirping birds splashing patterns of color against the dappled light of the mesh ceiling.

The Masker sweeps his arm out in an expansive movement. "This is my aviary. Here, I breed the songbirds that fly all over Noveskina."

"It—it's lovely," I say, bewildered. "But why are you bringing me here?"

"I want to let you hear for yourself. I have nightingales, thrushes, warblers, larks, and more, all living together. Listen to how pleasantly the sounds they make blend and complement one another."

Naturally, I grew up hearing the songbirds of Noveskina. Their singing is one of the things that makes our city such a delightful place. But I've never heard so many birds in one place before. The sweet, high notes of the nightingales are punctuated by the short, sharp staccatos of a blue jay. The birdsong *is* beautiful.

The Masker sighs. "I wish it could be this way for people. But it is not. In the old days, we didn't have voice control. People spoke out, gave their opinions, expressed themselves freely, all without restraint. This caused disharmony, disagreements. It was impossible to get anything accomplished. No one could ever agree on exactly what to do or how to go about it.

"Worse, when the discussions involved neighboring cities, with their strange customs and different values—the irritating tones! The harsh sounds of anger, mingling with high squeaks of fear. Whining self-pity mixed with roaring rage. Our voices did not blend harmoniously like the songs of my beautiful birds. Instead, these sounds caused arguments and, ultimately, war. Since the destruction, we have learned the importance of leadership. All voices must be given in service to the One Voice."

I nod impatiently, already knowing most of this. It is part of the history we all learn. "Of course we are nothing like birds," I venture.

"No," agrees the Masker. "We're not." He looks at me, his gaze kind. "That is why your mater will make you a servant's Mask. You will stay in my house until it is ready."

I bite my lip, knowing it is useless to argue. My eyes dart around the aviary, measuring the distance to the other side. Maybe I can escape—now.

"No, you can't run." The Masker's manner is hopelessly certain. "The screens in this aviary are stronger than they look. Besides, where would you go? I'd ask for you to be brought back if you escaped. People understand that I only speak for the good of Noveskina." The Masker eyes me carefully. "You do enjoy the unity in our city, don't you Miri?"

I nod. Of course I enjoy the unity. Who doesn't? It is the pride of the city: our One Voice. "But I don't understand why I must be a house servant in order for our city to remain united!"

"You've witnessed things only the Important Officials are ever allowed to see," he answers, his tone strict. "As an adult Noveskinian, you must submit your will to the needs of the community." He resumes his affable manner. "Anyway, it is not so bad being a house servant. I'm sure you'll get used to it. House servants are essential to our well-being. And they are free to go anywhere."

I clench my fists. *Yes, anywhere. In silence and waiting on other people.*

The Masker leads me back into the sharing room where the house servant has already laid out the evening meal. "Hungry?"

I shake my head. I can't eat a bite. My stomach rolls with nausea, and I feel like I might never be able to eat again. Come to think of it, it doesn't look like house servants eat much either. They are all thin.

Oblivious to my discomfort, the Masker digs into his meal. Finishing with a dessert of sugared snails, he gives a small, contented burp. Then he rings for his servant, completely ignoring the fact that I haven't touched my food.

I watch the girl curiously as she clears away the platters. She continues to make that peculiar sound, like a soft hum, in the back of her throat. I've never heard a house servant do anything like this before, but the Masker doesn't seem to notice anything out of the ordinary.

She is young, too. Not much older than me. She'd be pretty, with her glossy dark hair hanging down her back, if the skin on her face weren't drawn so taut.

"Where is my clarinet?" demands the Masker. "It is missing from the instrument room."

The servant stops humming. "I took it for cleaning. I'll put it back soon." She speaks with the hoarse whisper of all servants.

"I'm surprised how much maintenance these instruments seem to require," the Masker mutters.

The servant begins humming again.

"I'm going out for the evening, as usual," says the Masker, standing. "Watch Miri. She may enjoy the instruments. Talk to her. Keep her entertained. Just remember she's not to see or communicate with anyone but you. Understand?"

The humming stops just long enough for the servant to answer. "Yes, Masker."

"Good evening, Miri," says the Masker, giving me a slight nod before shuffling out of the room.

Maybe for you, I think bitterly. I can't understand why I'm being punished. What did I witness that was so bad? The Masking ceremony was strange, but Mater said everything went well. And I shouldn't be punished for seeing the forbidden instruments. After all, the Masker showed them to me himself. In any case, the people would understand his need to keep them. He guards us with the One Voice. Besides, I would never tell....

The servant leads me back to the music room. I can't take my eyes off her now that I've been threatened with her fate.

She stops the odd humming and a rosy glow blooms from her throat. Startled, I inhale sharply. She is a servant. Servants don't have enough voice to show Talent color, do they?

The color dims and dissipates. Puzzled, I rub my eyes. Perhaps I am only seeing spots.

She heads through the arched entry into the instrument room. Slipping away from her once her back is turned, I find the door that leads back into the tunnels. Furtively placing my palm against the recognition lock, I will it to let me out. But, naturally, it does no such thing. Turning from the lock, I see the servant standing in the hallway, watching me. She doesn't say anything as I follow her guiltily back to the music room.

As soon as we enter, she begins to tell me about the various instruments, holding them up one at a time to show me. She has deep circles under her eyes. "You look tired," I can't help saying. Patting the cushions next to me, I add, "Please sit down."

"It's not proper for servants to sit with their superiors," she says mechanically, but I catch her look of longing as she stares at the comfortable pillows.

"Go ahead," I urge. Despite being so strung up on fear, I'm amused to be allowed to converse with this house servant.

She sits down and stretches her legs out. "Ah! It does help to take the weight off my feet. Now, where was I?" She begins telling me about the guitar. Her voice sounds different than it did in front of the Masker. It is no longer flat and raspy.

She continues to speak, but I don't really listen. Her talking is a vague background to the thoughts tumbling through my mind. *If I can get a message to my parents, they will help. Certainly they won't let their daughter be Masked as a house servant. Pater would never allow it. They would be disgraced. Especially Mater.*

Suddenly, I stare at the servant. She is the answer! I must convince her to deliver a cube to my parents. Surely, Mater will refuse to make the servant's Mask if she knows it is for me. "What's your name?" I ask.

"You don't need to know that," she answers. "I'm just a house servant—"

"You don't understand!" I interrupt impatiently. "The Masker wants to make me a house servant, too."

The servant breaks all the rules of servant protocol and stares right at me, her gray eyes deepening with pity. Then she reaches for a skinny, silver instrument on the low table beside us. "I like the flute the best," she says softly, blowing a long, gorgeous pink and blue note, which soars into the room, doing melodic acrobatics across the ceiling.

"But you are Talented!" I exclaim.

"No," says the servant, moving over to the cello. She rubs a long stick back and forth on the strings until the instrument speaks in a mellow voice, a voice as comforting and golden as that of the Masker.

"Then how can you play like this?"

She shrugs. "This isn't a real Talent. It's not a deep soul gift, and it certainly hasn't come easily. It has taken me years of practice." She looks at me, and her eyes seem strangely familiar. "The Masker made me study the old music learning cubes so I could show him how to play the instruments he collected after the wars."

She sets the cello aside and beats out a series of sounds on the drums. "This is called a marching rhythm," says the servant. My foot taps in time, as I watch shots of green fill the room.

I want to ask her to take a cube to my parents right away, but I know it won't work to ask her just yet. Above all else, servants are obedient. I've heard that the Masks they wear are designed to keep them that way. She won't go against the Masker's wishes unless, maybe—I clutch at the frail hope—I can somehow make her my friend.

Sometimes servants do risk punishment for their loved ones. Once, our house servant actually left work without permission when his child was sick. And I've heard of others telling fibs to protect their spouses or hiding other house servants to help them avoid punishment.

Making friends with this servant is my only chance of escaping the awful fate of becoming one myself. But how am I to make friends with her? She won't even tell me her name.

I watch her carefully, searching for some clue to her personality. But she just drums on, her eyes unfocused, her thoughts elsewhere.

My heart sinks. To her, entertaining me is just another task.

The drum beats a monotonous rhythm into my skull. The march. It sounds ominous to me: ser-vant. Ser-vant. Ser-vant.

Chapter 10

A SURPRISING OFFER

LIGHT SLIPS THROUGH the canopy of creamy velvet that surrounds me. It is morning, and I open my eyes reluctantly, dreading this day.

The bells on the door jangle as the servant enters.

She hands me a cup of steaming broth. I take it and sip, watching her as she lays my cleaned ritual gown at the end of the bed. Her skin is smooth, and there isn't the slightest ripple where her Mask attaches at the base of her throat. She turns to me. "Would you like me to do your hair?"

I start to say no. I never do much with my hair beyond plaiting it into a single braid. But then I reconsider: "Yes, please." Having her do my hair might give me a chance to get to know her, to make friends with her.

After I finish my broth, she hands me a warm, moist cloth to wipe my face with. Then she brushes my hair with long, even strokes and begins the intricate braids that are the fashion in Noveskina.

"What's it like being a servant?" I ask.

She surprises me by answering. "You get used to it."

"I'll never get used to it!" I pick at the soft lounge cover. "I went to the elite training center. No one who graduates from there becomes a...a servant!"

I flush, suddenly aware of how tactless that sounded. I hope I haven't hurt her feelings. She doesn't seem to react as she calmly loops one braid on the side of my head and pins it in place. She begins another. "Well, you aren't part of your graduating class now that you've missed the bonding."

Taking a deep breath, I struggle to keep my voice steady. "I just don't understand why he won't let me wait and be bonded with the next group."

The servant sighs. "How would I know the Masker's mind?" She pins the last braid and then fastens a cowl of decorative netting over her handiwork in the fashion of upper class Noveskinian women. The servant hands me a piece of beaten and polished metal. Looking in it, I'm amazed at how elegant my red hair looks. "Thank you."

"At your service," she replies.

I don't know what to say. How will we ever become friends when she is so distant and formal?

"Morning meal is ready," she announces.

"Share it with me," I suggest spontaneously.

"It is not proper for a house servant to eat with non-servants," she recites woodenly, leading me down the hall to the sharing room.

"I'm practically a house servant myself, and I'm lonely. Please share a meal with me."

She looks around apprehensively, her gaze flickering over the sharing room furniture: thick, brocade cushions set beside a low table on the plush carpet. "I don't know...."

I speak fast. "The Masker already bent the rules by permitting you to converse with me."

She hesitates, and I press my advantage. "He said to do whatever it takes to keep me entertained."

"He did say that...."

"Can we eat in the garden?"

The servant squeezes her hands together. "I wish the Masker were here to ask."

"Oh, come on!" I point out the window to the flourishing, green garden. "How do we get out there?"

The servant leads me through a small door outside. Looking around, I see that there is no escape route from here; the garden is completely enclosed. But it is a pleasant place, with daffodils and tulips in bloom and rose bushes trained to grow flat against the tall fence.

The servant sets platters of food on a table under the leafy canopy of the trees. She waves a fat bumblebee away with her hand and begins the invocation: "We thank the earth for this food. We thank the Masker for the one song, one story, One Voice that gives us unity."

"We give thanks," I say automatically, filling my bowl with the honeyed beans. "How do you suppose the Masker manages to create unity?" I wonder.

The house servant mumbles something under her breath. It sounds like "steal."

"What?"

"Nothing," she replies, perching on the edge of her chair as if poised for flight.

I nibble on a candied leaf, studying her. She must be worried that she'll be accused of stealing if she is caught eating with me. "Don't worry," I say. "If the Masker finds us, I'll tell him that I ordered you to share a meal with me."

Perhaps this relaxes her because she helps herself to one spoonful of beans after another, eating swiftly and efficiently, as if she is starved. I watch for a while, wondering what house servants are fed and vowing that I'll save her the best tidbits from my meals—at least as long as I am stuck here. "I really wish you'd tell me your name."

She pauses for a second in her ravenous eating. "Melody."

"What an unusual name."

"It means a kind of song," she answers. "It's one of the old names, from before...."

She must mean from before the destruction, I think, munching my cookie. There are real walnuts in it. We hardly ever have those at home although the food we eat is better than most since our family earns many credits. I wonder what Darin and Mater and Pater are having for their morning meal. Probably flat bread and baked apples. Thinking about them brings my plan back to mind. *I have to get a message to them! Otherwise, Mater will never guess that the requested servant's Mask is for me.*

Melody sits back in her chair. There is a pleasant flush on her cheeks, and she appears almost content.

This is probably the best chance I'll get. "Melody, will you help me?"

"I'd like to, if I can."

"Can you take a cube to my parents?"

Melody grips the edges of her chair, her knuckles white.

"Please," I beg. "You won't even have to give it to them. Bring it to my brother, Darin, and they'll never even know who delivered it. Darin won't tell anyone, and he'll make sure they get it. Just tell him it's from me."

She frowns doubtfully.

"It's only a cube," I plead. "I know Mater and Pater will convince the Masker to change his mind if I can just get word to them."

She hesitates for the blink of an eye, as if she might agree, and then she lets out a long, sad sigh. "I can't. It's too dangerous. Do you know what they do to house servants who disobey?"

I shake my head. "What?"

The servant shudders.

Her refusal upsets me so much that I barely register the sound of the recognition lock, but there is no mistaking the distinctive limp of the Masker. Melody starts to hum and quickly stacks the two bowls together so that they look like one, but she isn't fast enough.

The Masker holds one hand behind his back and transfixes her with his glassy gaze. "What are you doing eating with Miri? She's not in your class yet! What is the meaning of this?" He frowns and Melody cringes. "I'll have you punished as soon as I finish with Miri."

Melody gives me a beseeching look.

"It's not her fault!" I protest. "I ordered her to share the meal with me. You told her to entertain me."

"I'll still have to punish her. She knows better. Servants are never allowed to eat with us."

I take a step forward. "No! It's not fair." Impulsively, I add, "Punish me instead!" Melody gasps.

The Masker tosses his head of glossy black curls back and laughs. "That isn't possible. You don't wear a servant's Mask," he says, revealing a ceramic bowl that he had kept hidden behind his back. "But tomorrow you will. And I will take you up on your offer then. Perhaps, after you've felt the punishment meted out to unruly house servants, you will be less quick to volunteer for it in the future."

He takes the lid off of the bowl and pulls something out of the liquid. My eyes bulge. It's a Mask. It looks like the Masks of my friends, but sharp prongs line one side of the flesh.

"Your mother made this especially for you. See what a lovely job she's done."

"No." I back away from the dangling Mask with its red-veined points. "She wouldn't make me a house servant's Mask! She wouldn't do it."

"She did indeed," the Masker answers with satisfaction. "Although I do admit that she was grieved when she learned you must be Masked as a servant. She and your pater were extremely upset." The Masker gives me a long look with his depthless black eyes. "I had to remind them both of the paramount importance of keeping the unity in Noveskina, no matter what personal sacrifices must be made."

His words fall like freezing hail around my ears, dashing the last of my hopes.

"At least," adds the Masker, "I was able to remind them that we still have hope for Darin. High hopes. He shows every sign of being immensely Talented. Perfect for the needs of Noveskina." He smiles at me. "That should be a comfort to you, too, Miri."

The Masker carefully returns the Mask—my Mask—to the ceramic bowl. "Because you are being Masked as a servant, there is no need for ceremony. Only the three of us will be in attendance," he says, gesturing to the servant. "We'll do it first thing in the morning."

The horror of his words hits me deep in my gut. It roils and builds, gathering force, until it bursts from me in a black, thunderous boom, and I hear it for a second before recognizing the sound of my own voice.

"NO!"

Flinching, the Masker quickly moves away from the force of

the sound. Then he straightens and raises his bushy eyebrows. "I can see that you would never have managed another year without a Mask. Your voice is already too strong."

My teeth sink into my lower lip until I taste blood. There is nothing, absolutely nothing, I can do to make him change his mind. Tomorrow I will be a servant. Me. The daughter of two of Noveskina's most Important Officials.

Tears fill my eyes, and I stumble past the Masker. I run to my sleeping chamber and collapse on the lounge. *They didn't even care enough to stop him! If only I hadn't spied on that ritual. If only I hadn't been caught. If only I had a Talent!* My deep sobs shake my shoulders.

Melody quietly walks into the room.

She sits on the edge of the lounge and rubs my neck. "That was a brave thing you did."

"What do they do to disobedient house servants?"

"I've never been punished before, but from what I've heard servant Masks respond to electrical currents. They dig into specific pressure points. They inflict pain."

I shudder. Those pointy prongs.

She bends down, hesitates, and then whispers in my ear. "There is one way to escape, but it's dangerous...."

Chapter 11

THE SCENT OF FREEDOM

"I'LL DO ANYTHING!"

"You won't be able to live in Noveskina anymore," she warns.

"But there's nowhere else to live—nothing left since the destruction." I look up at Melody. "Unless you mean the farms?"

The melancholy sound of the Masker playing the cello drifts into the room. Melody continues to knead the tense muscles in my neck. "Have you heard of the Secret Valley?"

My back stiffens. "Of course. But my teacher told us it was just a fable."

Melody snorts. "That's what the Masker would have people believe. But the Secret Valley is real enough."

Colored light shines out from the pink, plastic lamp. The soft color is supposed to help us unwind and relax. But I don't feel relaxed at all. I frown and barely notice Melody's deft fingers easing the pain at the base of my skull. "How come the Masker wouldn't want people to think it existed?"

"I think he doesn't want anyone to leave Noveskina. The population is too small as it is."

"Why would people leave?" I ask. "Noveskina is a wonderful place to live."

"Then why do you want to go?" she asks wryly.

I wince. Noveskina is obviously less wonderful to a house

servant, and I realize with sudden clarity that my life wouldn't be nearly so wonderful without them. "Who lives in the Secret Valley?"

"All sorts," answers Melody.

"How do you know? Have you been there?"

"Yes," says Melody. "Just tell me, do you want to go or not?"

"How do I get there? How would I cross the deadlands?"

She stops massaging. "I can help you get out of this house. And then, if you have somewhere to hide until evening, I can get you through the Wall. There is a way through the deadlands, trust me."

My eyes widen. "I can't go alone. The flyers have seen wild animals out there during surveillance. Come with me," I plead. "You won't have to be a servant anymore."

"I would if I could," she answers, sighing. "But there are reasons I must stay...." She draws a tiny, wrinkled piece of parchment from her apron pocket. "This is a map to the Secret Valley." Melody's eyes hold mine. "If you are caught, you have to promise to eat this map!"

"Eat it?"

"I made it small enough that it can be swallowed in one gulp. It's very important the Masker doesn't get hold of it. Promise?"

"Yes. I promise." A new worry crosses my mind. "But even if I find the Secret Valley, I won't know anyone when I get there."

"Give the map to the first people you meet. It will work as an introduction."

I frown. The old parchment seems like a flimsy thing on which to base my hopes.

Melody's eyes are luminous with sympathy. "It's either that or be Masked as a servant tomorrow."

I can't answer. If I leave, I might never see Darin, Jalene, and my age-mates again. Or my parents. Thinking of the Mask that Mater made me, I flinch. *Would I even want to see my parents again?*

The silence stretches out. Sunlight shines through the ivy outside making shifting patterns on the windowpane.

If I stay here, I'll be a house servant for the rest of my life. No one even speaks to house servants, except to issue commands. *I won't have my parents. I won't have my brother. I won't have my friends.* I think of the pinching prongs of a servant's Mask and wince. "What will the Masker do to you if he finds out you helped me escape?"

"I'm good at playing innocent. He'll never know I had a thing to do with it," Melody says confidently. "Don't worry about me."

My forehead tightens in a frown. "But he expects you to watch me, and when I disappear, he's going to blame you."

Melody gives me a confident smile. "I have a foolproof plan, Miri. But I can't tell you in case he *listens* to you and overhears it. Now, make up your mind. Will you go?"

"Yes," I answer, resigned. "I have nothing to lose."

"Then we'll have to go now," Melody says briskly, "while the Masker is practicing his music."

A tremor sweeps my body. "Now?"

Melody doesn't say anything. Instead, she opens the antique wooden wardrobe and picks out a pair of walking sandals. They are made from the salvaged rubber of old tires. Then she opens a drawer and pulls out my gown and a hooded brown cloak to cover it. Last, she reaches for a small backpack hanging off of a hook inside the wardrobe door. "Get dressed," she orders, holding the pack. "I'll run down to the cooking room and fill this with supplies."

I barely have time to dress and lace my sandals before Melody returns with a bulging pack. "Let's go—but be quiet."

We slip out of the door and tiptoe down the thickly-carpeted hall. The Masker is still playing—it's a mournful tune. I follow Melody down to the entryway. She places her hand on a shiny green recognition lock. It lets us through. We step forward into darkness and the door closes behind us. Blinking, I try to see ahead. I am back in the tunnels.

"Follow the scent of lemon," directs Melody. "You'll come out in a safe place. Then go hide until nightfall." She pauses and grips my hand in farewell.

My hand trembles.

"Cheer up," admonishes Melody. "You might have a companion on the other side of the Wall, although I can't guarantee it."

"Who?"

"I don't want to tell you more than you need to know now, just in case you are caught and questioned. You'll just have to wait and see. If he's still there, I'm sure it'll be quite a surprise—hardly what you're expecting—but he'll recognize you by the smell of me on your clothes."

"Is smell his Talent?"

Melody chuckles quietly. "I guess you could say that."

The soft sounds of the cello end. "Quick," says Melody. "Before he starts listening and hears our thoughts. Where will you hide? I'll meet you there before dark."

I hesitate. I've never told anyone where my sanctuary is, but it really is the perfect hiding place. And I'll never get through the Wall without Melody's help.

I give her directions. Then I remember that she won't have me to help her through. "How will you get past the seal?"

"A little humming can work wonders."

I stare at Melody blankly. Her cheeks dimple in a mysterious smile, but she doesn't explain. "Go," she says. "And don't forget to stick with the lemon."

There is a brief flash of light when she opens the door out of the tunnel. She gazes at me for a moment in farewell, and the expression in her gray eyes jogs my memory. Suddenly, I know why she looks familiar. Melody is the house servant Jalene and I saw that day at the Wall. "Wait!" I cry, full of questions.

But she has already gone. I am alone in the dark.

I shiver as my mind races. *Who is she really? Can I trust her? What will happen if the Masker catches me now? I can't go back. And I can't get through the recognition door, even if I do change my mind.* Smells drift around me in a fragrant potpourri: lavender, mint, pine.... Sniffing, I locate the zingy, lemon aroma and take a step, holding my arms out in front of me to feel the walls of the tunnel, following it deeper into the dark.

The only sounds I hear are my breath and my sandals squeaking as I walk on the hard floor. At first it is easy to follow the lemon. The smell is so strong that it beckons to me like the warmth of the sun.

But as I walk further into the pitch black, the tunnels branch out, and many more smells mingle together, competing with the tangy smell of lemon. Inhaling carefully, I follow the delicious scent. Then I stop. This isn't lemon. It's orange.

My stomach knots. What if I can't find the lemon again? *Don't think that!* I tell myself, turning and following the path back the way I came. At least I hope it is back the way I came. It is impossible to tell in the dark. And my sense of smell is growing jaded and fatigued. I cannot let that happen. Not here. I could end up wandering the tunnels forever, or accidentally stumbling into the crypt.

If I blunder into the crypt in the dark, no one will find me until the next burial! I panic. I spin around. I sniff frantically, breathless, and almost faint with fear.

Suddenly the darkness seems like a large and heavy thing. I can no longer breathe from the weight of it on my chest.

"Help!" I call desperately. The sound of my own voice echoes away and back at me from every direction. My mouth goes dry.

Crazy with terror and dizzy with smells, I force myself to stay still. If I don't calm down, I really will get lost. I sit down and close my eyes. Inhaling and exhaling slowly, I use breath meditation to bring my thoughts inward and sort through my fears. A sense of calm comes over me, and I feel myself breathing freely again. Then, opening my mouth, I try tasting the scents on my tongue. Is that a trace of lemon? I inhale cautiously. Yes. Definitely lemon.

I stand and take a step closer to the scent. Then another. With each step I take, the lemon trail grows stronger, more robust and, at last, unmistakable. Following my nose, I smell eagerly, my feet picking up speed as I practically race down the lemon tunnel. I can't wait to get out of the dark. To be free.

After what seems like years, I see a green light glowing at the end of the tunnel. I race toward it. Shrubs. Moving aside the brambles, I peer out. Neatly trimmed hedges, stately trees, clipped grass...the park!

Choosing caution, I stay slightly hidden as I look around. The first thing I see is Darin streaking by in a race with a group of his friends. My heart jumps. It feels like years since I last saw my brother; so much has happened since my Masking day. I want to run after him—catch him—tell him everything; but if

I didn't know his Talent was command, I'd think it was racing. He runs by so quickly that I don't stand a chance of catching him discreetly.

And there is a circle of my friends. They talk quietly under the oaks, still celebrating their Masking. By next week, they will be given their job assignments and will begin their training. It is hard to believe we were together only yesterday. My heart aches to be with them.

I watch my age-mates for a while. There is something different about them, but I can't quite figure it out. Eris chats to Nonce, who is petting a rabbit. I turn my gaze to Ceiron. He looks calm and collected, as usual. But he seems to be talking more than listening. I scan the group, looking for Jalene, but I pause when I see Aron. He is sitting quietly, for once.

For a moment I wish he could somehow save me from being Masked as a servant. Save me from having to leave Noveskina. I can't help remembering Jalene's old tales of chivalrous knights and swooning ladies. But of course, those are just stories. Aron wasn't even friendly the last time I saw him. But at least his tumbling can make me laugh. And I could use a good laugh.

Besides, I'm dying to talk to my friends.

It's a risk to be out in public, but I'm going to take the chance. I'll have to come out sooner or later anyway to get to my sanctuary in time to meet Melody.

I take a deep, fortifying breath, hoping my friends don't know that I'm not supposed to be here. I walk over and give them all a huge smile. "Hi, everybody!"

They all stare at me.

No one says a word.

Chapter 12

ALONE

I **GATHER MY** courage and break the uncomfortable silence. "Where's Jalene?"

Eris stands solidly on the ground, staring at me without the hint of a smile. I shift nervously. "She's coming," she answers finally, pointing.

My gaze follows her finger over to a group of babies, playing with their multi-colored stacks of learning cubes, and younger children eagerly practicing Talents. Three instructors talk to each other as they casually watch over the kids. Jalene is weaving her way through the busy park scene toward our group.

"Jalene!" I call.

Jalene speaks softly, giving me a puzzled look. "Miri? I thought you were supposed to be with the Masker."

"That's what the Training Instructor told us," interjects Eris tonelessly.

Summoning my wits, I fib, "It's okay. The Masker said I could spend the afternoon in the park. He's going to Mask me tomorrow." I give them a big, fake smile.

My friends nod. "That's fine, Miri." But their voices are blank.

I am dying to spend a little time with them. This might be the last time I see the group. There are still hours and hours left until nightfall when Melody is due to meet me. "Do you want to do something together?" I ask. "I mean, since I have the afternoon free and all."

Eris clears her throat. "I don't know, Miri. We're awfully busy trying to adjust to being Masked...."

"It takes a lot of energy," whispers Nonce. She sets the rabbit down and watches for a second as it hops off through the tall grass. Then she turns away, disinterested.

"Why?" I ask.

Aron shrugs. "It's not something we can explain. You wouldn't understand anyway."

That hurts. "I'll just stay with you and watch," I say, straining to keep the sadness out of my voice.

"There's nothing to watch!" snaps Aron.

"What about your tumbling?" I ask desperately. Nothing seems to be the same with my friends.

Aron gives a sharp toss of his head, flicking his blond hair out of his eyes. "I'm not in the mood."

"Is something wrong? Are you all mad at me?" I ask.

"It's not you, Miri. We are just different, now," says Eris solemnly. "We're bonded."

I can't say anything to that. Instead, I focus my eyes on a bright pink learning bubble that floats over from the nearby children's group. I watch it slowly form the letters of the alphabet, as if it is the most interesting thing in the world. My eyes are dry when I finally look back at the group.

"Jalene?" I can't quite keep the pleading note out of my voice. "You'll walk with me, won't you?"

Jalene smoothes her gown. The purple isn't quite as deep and vivid as I remember, but perhaps that is because the outside light is brighter. "Okay, Miri," she agrees, moving away from the group. "But not far. I'm awfully tired."

That reminds me. "Do you remember how tired and old the Masker looked during the ritual?" I ask as soon as we are out of earshot of the others. If she remembers, maybe I can tell her what I saw: how he recharged himself and became young.

Jalene shakes her head. "Of course not. He's always young. Everyone knows that."

I chew my thumbnail. Jalene *had* noticed how old he was at the Masking. She said something. I heard her.

We amble further out of the group's hearing, and I ask the thing that is bothering me the most. "Jalene, what's going on with everyone? Is it something I've done?"

Jalene stops and looks at me. She reaches her hand out toward mine, but she pulls back before actually touching. Her brown eyes struggle with something, sparkling intensely and then veiling over in a confused cloud. At last, all she says is, "No. You haven't done anything. You're just different from us now. I'm sorry, Miri."

"That's not all!" I cry. "I can tell. You have more to say to me. Please, just say it!"

Jalene opens and closes her mouth as if she is fighting to speak. Her Mask seems to tighten around her throat, almost choking her so that she splutters and coughs. At last, she just shakes her head and wipes a tear from the corner of her eye.

I blink back my own tears. I knew I'd lose all my friends if we weren't bonded. I just didn't know how much it would hurt. "Will you tell me a story?" I ask, hoping to get a glimpse of the old, wonderful Jalene.

"No. I only tell stories for performances now."

I gape. Jalene *always* told stories. She told them when she was happy, or sad, or whenever she felt like it—which was practically all the time.

Jalene turns back to the group—her group. "I have to go now, Miri. I'll see you some other time." She gives me an airy wave as if this is nothing and I have not been her dearest friend for the past seven years. And then she walks away.

My face flushes—then chills cold as ice. If only Jalene realized this would be the last time we'd see each other. She'd never treat me like this...would she? I want so much to tell her *everything*—that I am running away, and why. But I know I can't confide in anyone—not even her. If what I tell her slips out, the Masker will find me.

Walking slowly away from my friends, I realize nothing is the same. Nothing will ever be the same. I look around for Darin, possibly the last person left who might be happy to see me. He is nowhere to be found. I wonder if he has gone home.

My feet tread the broken pavement, and I consider heading home myself. I want to pick up a few of my belongings, like the crystal necklace Jalene gave me for my last name day. It sparkles a rainbow of brilliant colors. And my favorite learning cube—the one that shows artists at work; you can look inside and watch the miniature people while they paint, or sculpt. Of course, it is just a moving three-dimensional picture—there aren't actually shrunken people in the cube as I believed when I was younger. And I want to get my class picture from last year. Last year, when I was still sure I'd discover my Talent and be just as happy as the rest of my classmates.

But most of all I want to find Darin and say goodbye. What will he think of my disappearance? The house will be so lonely for him without me. My jaw clenches. I don't want to leave. Noveskina is my home.

But then I remember the house servant, Melody. I recall the way she spoke to the Masker in that dull, tired tone; the way she got up early and stayed up late; the way she cooked and cleaned, but hardly ate. That is no life for me. If I go home, they will catch me. I cannot return. I decide to make my way to my sanctuary.

Heading down the back alley, through the overgrown dandelions, I'm relieved that, as usual, no one is around. Because of Noveskina's small population, there are many deserted buildings and unused areas. My teacher told us that in the old days it wasn't easy for people to find a spot to be alone. But now there are many places to go.

The buildings loom tall and impressive, despite their chipped paint. A few pigeons scatter out of my way, but otherwise it is quiet except for the scrunch of my sandals. Smelling the musty odor that always seems to linger here in the shadows between buildings, I turn to follow a small, dirt road.

Only two dozen paces away, the buildings are much smaller, and sunbeams warm the backs of my shoulders. At last, I see what I am looking for: a long, squat structure with a domed roof at the center. I don't hesitate to go in past the rotted wooden door, barely hanging from its copper hinges. This place is almost as familiar to me as the training center. I've spent so many days here searching for my deep soul gift.

The roof is half off the hallway and debris crunches under my feet, but I don't look. It is just the usual: dead bugs, feathers, leaves, and gritty dirt deposited by the blowing winds.

My presence disturbs the bats, and they dart around my head. "It's only me," I say, and perhaps the night creatures understand; they settle back in their roosts, hanging upside down from the beams. Continuing through the unlit corridor, I reach a sharp bend and face an antique mahogany door. I push on it, and it opens into a circular room. My sanctuary.

As I inhale deeply, the feeling of safety and peace flows

through me. No one will disturb me now. A slanted shaft of afternoon sun beams through the large hole in the ceiling. Craning my neck, I admire the unbroken part of the ceiling where faded frescoes picture Noveskina—or the city it used to be—before the wars: tall, rectangular buildings reach to the sky and dazzle the eyes with light reflected off their glass panes. Large roads crisscross through the city, filled with vehicles of all shapes and sizes. There are even flying transports in the air. It's amazing to see because, for lack of the lost technologies, we now walk everywhere in Noveskina. People in the fresco drive vehicles, fly, hold babies, laugh, talk, and play what I now know are the forbidden instruments. They are oblivious to the coming destruction and what it will mean.

I sit down in my favorite corner—the one with the soft moss growing through the cracked marble floor. It makes a comfortable cushion. A fat frog croaks and I smile. We've spent a lot of time together. He thrusts his chest out gaily at me and hops into the pool of rainwater that has filled a slight indentation in the settled floor. Now there is nothing to do but wait for Melody.

Opening the pack she gave me, I pull out some dried crabapples and sweetened pinesap and nibble a bit. Then I lie back against the moss and close my eyes.

Pictures of my friends shuffle through my head. *Why were they all so tired? They should have been happy and celebrating after being Masked. They've become real adults!*

Shivering beneath my warm cloak, I picture Aron's unnatural stillness. And I've never known him to snap at anyone before. Nonce was missing her usual halo of songbirds, and Ceiron hadn't noticed when I lied about the Masker giving me the day off. Eris was planted to the ground, and Jalene...Jalene wouldn't even tell me a story!

And she said we were different. Jalene and I have always been so much alike that we could finish each other's sentences.

Sadness sinks like a stone in my belly. It is too heavy and deep for me to cry. My body feels bruised with sorrow and exhaustion. Dozing off into a fretful sleep, my head is filled with flitting images and nightmares. Mater plucks an eyeless Mask out of the vat. The Masker chases me with a squirming piece of flesh.

I'm lost in the tunnels.

When I wake it is already dark—and chilly. I tie the hood of my thick wool cloak about my head and take a sip of water from my rations.

Deep shadows gather in the room. Where is Melody? She should be here by now.

Chapter 13

STRANGE COMPANION

I **GET UP** and cross the room, counting my steps: one, two, three, four...up to forty-seven. Then I turn and walk the other way. I crack my knuckles nervously, a habit I gave up years ago because the sound irritated Mater so much.

It is night now. But fortunately, it is not completely dark. The rising moon lights the sky. Still, Melody promised she'd be here before nightfall.

I am so worried that it takes a few minutes for my brain to register what my ears clearly hear—the patter of feet on marble. Someone is coming. Slipping into the shadows away from the moonlight, I strain my ears, listening. A soft hum of rosy light carries through the air, and I know it is Melody.

Melody pokes her head through the doorway. "Miri?" she calls softly.

"Finally!" I run over and throw my arms around her.

Even by the soft silvery light, I see Melody's blush. She gently disentangles my arms from her body. "There's no time to waste. I have to get right back. The Masker's not going out tonight as he normally does. He's staying home to prepare for your ritual, and he wants me to help. The only way I got out was by telling him I had to pick up more medication for you. Sometimes when children are very upset about being Masked,

their faces get too stiff, and it takes a bit more of the relaxant."
She tugs on my arm. "Let's go!"

Grabbing my pack, I follow her. We leave so fast that I
forget to turn and say good-bye to my sanctuary although I will
never see it again. There is no time. No time for anything but
this breathless run through the night.

It's hard to keep up with Melody. I can't tell where we are.
Melody drags me down an overgrown lane. Then she pulls me
up a steep hill. Scenery blurs and the air feels suddenly warm.
When we stop, we are in front of the Wall.

The spot looks familiar, but that isn't too surprising since
the Wall is one long, flat surface that extends the entire
perimeter of Noveskina. What is surprising is that there is
somebody already here. The figure sits with her back turned to
us, wearing a long, silk gown that shines as violet as Ceiron's
eyes in the moonlight. My heart beats faster. "Jalene?"

The figure turns, and my heart dances seeing that it is my
friend. We'll get to say good-bye after all! Pulling my hand out
of Melody's, I move closer to Jalene.

She looks at me, stares at Melody, and then she looks
back at me. "You broke your promise," she says in her flat adult
voice. "You betrayed my sanctuary to someone else—a-a
house servant!"

"I didn't! You don't understand—"

"How *could* you?" cries Jalene. Emotion makes her voice
crack through the Mask. The moon illuminates her skin. Her
flesh seems to bubble just at the hairline below her temples.
Jalene winces, as if in pain, and then she turns and runs. She
doesn't once look back at me.

"Wait! Jalene! It's not what you think," I yell. "Please come
back. I'll explain." My mouth tastes salty, the way it does when

I'm about to throw up. I turn to Melody. "This is where she's been coming for years and years. This is her sanctuary—the place where she discovered her storytelling Talent." *And she thinks I've betrayed her. And I'll never see her again. Never have a chance to explain.*

Melody pulls on my arm, shaking me from my thoughts. "There is no time for this. I have to get you through the Wall and then I must return to the Masker. Do you still have the map?" Melody stares at me, and her eyes remind me of a question I had been meaning to ask. "Why do you use this door? Jalene and I saw you the other day."

"It's the only door that isn't monitored. I think the Masker has forgotten it exists," she explains briefly. "Now be sure to stick right behind me when I open the recognition lock. You have to get out before it has time to register a second person."

I follow confidently. Darin and I practiced sneaking in recognition doors behind each other hundreds of times.

"This lock is more sensitive than the ones in private dwellings," warns Melody. "You have to stay right up against my back." She places her palm on a small, indented place in the Wall.

"House servant here," intones the lock. The Wall moves to reveal a narrow opening, and we go through. I'm glued so tightly to her back that we must seem like one very lumpy person. The door closes immediately after we slip past.

"Stick with the path. Check your map. You should reach the Secret Valley in three days," says Melody. She thrusts an instrument at me. "And take this." She looks at me steadily with her gray eyes. "Be sure you don't lose it. It's important. Understand?"

I carefully stow the long, silver tube into the inner chest

pocket of my gown. "But...why?"

"It's a complicated story, and I don't have time to tell it. Right now you need to go."

Melody places her hand on the Wall.

"Wait!" I cry. "Melody, are you sure you'll be safe?"

She smiles enigmatically. "He hasn't caught me yet."

"You've helped people escape before?"

She shakes her head. "Not exactly. But I am good at fooling him. He can't hear my thoughts."

"But what will you tell him about me? He'll know I had help escaping."

"I guess there is no harm in telling you now. I'm going to tell him that his life partner returned and ran off with you."

"The Masker has a life partner?"

"Yes. But she left him years ago. Still, he knows that's the sort of thing she might do. He'll believe me."

A relieved sigh shudders through my body. "Good luck, Melody."

"Good luck to you, as well," she replies before pressing the recognition lock.

"House servant here," repeats the mechanical voice.

And she is gone.

My eyes dart around as I warily take in my surroundings. This side of the Wall is coated with a shiny, sound-reflective material. I can see patches where the silvery substance is wearing off, but the structure still seems solid and strong. Of course, the city is unprotected from the inside, but there the Masker protects us with the One Voice.

Surprisingly, the land out here isn't dead at all. It is overgrown with blackberry bushes and thistles and grass so tall it reaches my waist. A narrow track leads through the bracken.

Looking around, I search eagerly for the companion Melody said might be here. But my heart sinks. There is no one.

I am alone on the wrong side of the Wall.

At least the brightness of the full moon makes it easy to see. Shifting my pack to a more comfortable position and wishing it weren't so heavy, I start an automatic prayer to the Masker to guide me well. I pause, realizing the irony of the gesture, and stop praying. My feet trample the faint path of bent grass, and I try not to prick myself on the thistles. If only I could fly like Eris; this would be no problem. I would soar right over the blackberry thorns, straight to the Secret Valley. Of course, if I had flying Talent, I would never have needed to leave Noveskina in the first place.

A bird I've never heard before breaks the eerie silence, hooting from a tree. Another one calls back. I can barely see the path through the grass, but it is the only one, so there is no risk of getting lost. At least, not yet.

Something rustles in the bushes up ahead. Goose bumps prickle my arms. *A dangerous animal?*

Shoving that thought down, I force my feet to continue stepping forward. The rustling stops. *Probably just the wind.* My mind wanders as I pick my way through the wilderness: *what will the Secret Valley be like? What will the people be like? What if they don't accept me? Where will I go then?*

Stop thinking! I tell myself. Every single thought only leads me to a new worry. *Just walk!* Which I do for all of three steps. Then I freeze, picturing Darin and the expression on his face once he learns I've run away. I wish for the hundredth time that I could have said good-bye. And what about Jalene, who was right there at the Wall? I curse under my breath at our misunderstanding and recall the strange way her skin sizzled in anger. It seemed to hurt her.

Something rubs against my heels.

Instinctively, I bolt, not caring that unseen thorny branches whip past, stinging my cheeks as I run. I can hear an animal panting as it chases me. And it's gaining! Turning, I fling my pack straight at the beast.

The large animal—it comes almost up to my hips—stops and sniffs the pack for a minute. Then it opens its mouth and lets out the most bloodcurdling howl. Moonlight makes its sharp teeth glisten.

I don't stick around to watch.

Facing forward, I hurtle down the trail, the silver instrument in my pocket banging against my chest. The beast follows, making strange yelping noises. Its large feet pad behind me; its hot breath on my heels. I pray, even though I don't know who I'm praying to anymore. "I don't want to die like this!"

I consider clubbing the animal with the metal instrument. But I don't think it is enough of a weapon to deal with those fangs. I keep running. But I am not fast enough. The beast leaps, knocking me to the ground and pinning me beneath its body. Writhing on the prickly earth, I try to get out, but the creature is too strong. It is heavy and seems to weigh nearly as much as me. It opens its mouth, and I shut my eyes, unable to bear the idea of watching it devour me.

A rough, sandpaper tongue slobbers all over my face. Cautiously opening one eye, I peer at the strange animal. *Does it have to wash me before it takes a bite?*

Its body is sturdy and compact, rippling with muscles. It has a big, funny, black nose, and paws for feet. The ears perk straight up. A long tail waggles back and forth from its russet-colored rump.

Propping myself up on my elbows, I stare into the creature's topaz eyes. They are just like the eyes that peered out of the vines the day that Jalene and I first encountered Melody. Suddenly, the animal doesn't look ferocious at all. In fact, the creature rolls onto its back with all four legs sticking straight into the air. He gives me a hopeful look.

He is in such an unguarded position with his belly exposed that I can't help but laugh out loud. "What do you want?" I ask, mentally reviewing all the mostly extinct animals I studied in school. I think of cheetahs, cougars, tigers, bobcats.... No, there is nothing feline about this creature. He is more likely canine, a wolf or coyote, although he is too hairy to be either of those.

"Woof!" says the animal.

In a flash, I recall the sound from my learning cube. This is a bark, and therefore the animal must be a dog. My shoulders relax. This animal won't hurt me. In the old days, they even kept dogs as household pets. The definition I memorized comes back to me perfectly: *Dog—any of a large and varied group of domesticated animals related to the fox, wolf, or jackal. Banned from Noveskina after the sound wars because of an uncontrollable tendency to make dissonant and dangerous sounds. See howling, barking.*

I scratch the soft fur of the animal's underbelly. He lies perfectly still with an almost blissful expression in his eyes. "I guess you're not going to eat me," I whisper, "so I'd better go back and find my pack. I doubt I'll make it for three days without supplies."

The dog follows me back and waits patiently while I hoist my pack onto my shoulders. As soon as I begin walking, he bounds along with me. We hike for a long time, fighting the dense brush that grows out of the blackened land on either side of the thin track. The branches bite and scratch my ankles, even ripping a hole in my cloak. Even so, we seem to be going at a good pace. My sandals squish steadily in the mud, and the dog pants beside me.

As we walk, the moon sinks in the sky. Hours pass. Slowly, the landscape begins to change from scraggly shrubs to the remnants of an old forest, leveled long ago. There is an occasional giant redwood remaining like a lonely sentinel. The tree stumps are huge and look monstrous in the moonlight, but I'm relieved to be back out in the open. My body feels looser as I inhale the cool air that flows through the field.

Something stirs in the underbrush.

In an instant, the dog is gone.

Chapter 14

A FEROCIOUS BEAST

FOR A WHILE, I wait. But the dog doesn't come back. Looking around nervously, I call softly, "Rrrf! Rrrf!" trying to speak his language, hoping the dog will return. The words sound ghostly falling into the quiet night.

After some time, I give up and hike on through the bleak landscape, my heart even heavier than before. Half an hour later, when I've completely given up on ever seeing the dog again, he slinks out of the undergrowth whimpering.

"What is it?"

He looks back at the trail. We've come so far that the looming wall surrounding Noveskina is barely visible in the distance. The dog whines and pads a few feet off the path, turning back and gazing at me expectantly.

"What's wrong?" I ask.

He runs behind an enormous old tree stump, emerges again in a second, and waits for me.

I walk up to the stump. The dog slips right inside the hollow core and then looks at me. Poking my head inside, I wonder what this strange animal wishes to show me.

It is surprisingly spacious inside this rotted old stump. The air smells musty, and soft lichens and mosses grow in the crevices and crannies of the reddish colored wood.

The dog thumps his tail on the powdery duff, looking so eager for me to join him that I can't resist. There is plenty of room inside the stump for both of us to sit comfortably, and I am tired and hungry. A little rest won't hurt. I take my pack off and shove it in first. Then, crawling on all fours, I wiggle into the hollow core. I lie back against the contoured inside of the dead tree, stretching my legs out in the moist earth.

Digging in my pack, I pull out some dried, boneless fish. After a few bites, the pleading look in the dog's eyes gets to me, and I toss him a chunk, which he quickly gulps down.

A voice pierces the still night air. *Melody's companion!* Sitting up, I open my mouth to shout, "I'm here!" But before the sound fully passes my lips, the dog knocks me over and lies across my face and chest, muffling my cry.

"Did you hear that?" hisses a male voice.

"Sounded like a person. She must be out here somewhere," answers a female. "The Masker said she can't have gone far yet."

My bones go limp as pudding as I lie shivering under the animal's thick fur.

The voices continue. "I can't believe anyone would run away from Noveskina."

"Me either," agrees the male voice. "It's creepy out here...too quiet, no people, nothing to eat...and who knows what kind of wild animals are lurking about."

"Let's find her fast, before we run into one," the female says fearfully.

Cowering underneath the dog, I inhale his odor of damp fur. There is silence.

"There's a track here!" calls the male searcher.

"Look!" shouts the female. "A piece of a cloak."

Please don' t let them find me....

"We'll find her before the flyers. They won't be out searching until the morning," says the woman. "Think how the Masker will reward us when we do."

"Credits would be nice. For nicer living quarters. And perhaps some of those newfangled heat lights. I was chilly last winter."

"I'd like passes to more performances. The group just Masked has great Talents," says the woman. "It'd be nice to see them while they are still fresh and strong."

"This way," directs the man.

Their footsteps break the twigs right outside my hiding place. My heart stops beating.

Suddenly the glare of a globe light beams into the stump. I shrink underneath the dog as he begins a low snarl. I can imagine the reaction of the searchers as they see Woof's fangs for the first time.

"Back up!" orders the man. "There's an animal in there."

The dog continues to growl a sustained and threatening rumble from the back of his throat.

The light from the globe vanishes. I listen to the snap of nearby roots and branches as the two searchers hurry away from the cut-off trunk. The man's voice comes from farther away, "She can't be in there with that beast—unless it ate her!"

"Serves her right if it did," grumbles the woman. "After putting us through a night like this."

"Come on. We're wasting time. Let's look closer to the footpath."

I don't move. Instead, I strain my ears, listening to their receding footsteps. Long after the sound of their voices drifts away, I lie still. At last, the shaggy dog moves off of me, and I can breathe again. I don't say anything; I just watch him with his ears perked up, listening. Did this dog protect me on purpose?

Finally he nudges me with his hot muzzle and stands up. "Are they gone?" I whisper.

The dog walks out of the tree trunk and sniffs the air. He is always sniffing something. Suddenly, Melody's words come back to me: "I'm sure he'll recognize you by the smell of me on your clothes." This dog must be Melody's companion. And thank the Masker he is—otherwise I'd have been caught for sure. "You know," I say to the dog, "the learning cubes said that people used to name their dogs in the old days. I'm going to have to think of something to call you."

"Woof," he barks.

"Woof?" I ask. "Is that your name?"

The dog doesn't answer. He just takes a few paces and then turns around, waiting for me. "Well, I'll call you Woof anyway," I say, shouldering my pack and following him back out into the night.

Time seems to pass slowly as we plod through the nightmarish landscape tense and in silence. It gives me the creeps the way the giant stumps cast surreal shadows on the ground. The *whoosh whoosh whoosh* of a night bird flapping high above makes me want to duck for cover. In the city, the sounds of street sweepers, time criers, and early flyers regularly punctuate the darkness—unlike this *whoosh*, which is the only noise that breaks the eerie night quiet.

Eventually we emerge from the destroyed forest into a clearing. It is easier walking, and I don't have to worry about wild things pouncing on me from the brush. But I am more visible, too. Glancing nervously at the sky, I check for the early morning flyers the searchers mentioned. But it is still dark, and everything is quiet except for the occasional birdcall. Hopefully, by morning, I'll be too far away for the flyers to find me. Flying is tiring, and they can only go a few miles beyond the Wall before they must turn back and rest.

As I walk, the clearing becomes increasingly black and charred. These must be the real deadlands. Here, there is no new growth to camouflage what the wars have done. Sickened, I step into the bleakness where nothing grows. Woof whimpers, and I will myself to walk faster even though I am miserably tired.

The moon has almost set, so it is hard to see the large shapes that thrust up from the ground. Squinting, I wonder. Metal? Maybe these are the old missile silos. In the old days people knew how to condense and store the energy from sound. The Training Instructor said that the Talent energy expressed in individual voices was the most powerful when used this way. And, of course, the second most powerful energy was created by the forbidden instruments. Together they created the destruction.

Shuddering, I tell myself to keep moving quickly even though I am stumbling from exhaustion. The distance across the charred land is wider than it appeared, and the sky is beginning to brighten. Afraid of being seen, I break into a light jog. The heavy pack slaps against me, making my back ache. I run for nearly half an hour. By the time we reach a break in the ruined earth, my lungs and legs are burning, and my mind is numb.

Relief swells in my heart when my feet step once more upon living grass. I lay down my brown traveling cloak and collapse upon it. Looking up at the sky, I see the first pale peach streaks of dawn glow. A strange and distant roaring fills the air like wind in the trees, only it isn't windy. I pull out my water container and take a sip. The dog whines as he watches me, so

I pour a little into my palm and let him lap it up.

Woof stretches and walks over to a boulder and pees against its side. The dog has the right idea. I copy him, modestly hiding behind a willow tree. I smile at the ridiculousness of hiding from a dog. He certainly didn't hide from me!

"Where are we?" I ask, coming out from behind the tree and unfurling my map.

Woof doesn't answer. He curls up at the base of the willow tree, tucks his tail between his legs, and closes his eyes. Some help.

I trace the path I took—there is the brambly area close to the Wall, followed by the tree stumps, and, yes, the burned earth...then there is a small forest.

I glance around. We are in a meadow. There is no forest in sight. Did I take a wrong turn coming through the deadlands?

My thighs start to itch. I scratch hard. There is no way I want to retrace my steps through those exposed fields—especially not with morning coming and the danger of flyers with it.

Running my finger over the black line on the map that indicates the trail, I note that it heads down a steep slope and stops at a wavy blue line. Water?

The trail resumes on the other side of the blue line. If I can find the water, then maybe I can follow it to get back to the track. Chewing a handful of candied carrots, it occurs to me that the noise in the air does sound a bit like the canals of Noveskina after a heavy rain. Can it be water?

My eyes sting from weariness, and I can hardly keep them open as I follow the roaring sound down a slope to a torrentially flowing river. Here the noise is so loud that it drowns my thoughts. The water isn't blue at all. More mud-colored with frothy whitecaps. The river churns, flinging itself over rocks in a thick spume. Holding a hand up to shade my eyes, I scan the opposite bank for any sign of a trail.

There is nothing.

I look down the river. Is that a bridge? I squint. No. Just a fallen log.

Standing on tiptoe, I look far up the river.

A sky-blue gown flaps high in the morning sky. *A flyer!*

Chapter 15

A RAGING TORRENT

AS I RACE across the mossy rocks trying to find cover, my sandals squeak on a wet fern and sink into the sand. I lose my balance and tumble down the steep embankment. Branches and sharp rocks scrape my face and arms. With a splash, I plunge into the river. The icy water takes my breath away. Spray fills my nostrils. Spluttering, I flail my arms, looking for something to grab. *Anything!*

I inhale water and choke. Legs bash against rocks. Pain shoots up my shin. My ears ring. Currents grab me and smash my left shoulder into a jagged boulder in the center of the river. I cling desperately, panting. Woof barks madly as he runs up and down the shore, but I can barely hear him over the roar of the water. I know I have to think of some way to get out of the water before I freeze or drown, but my mind is numb and blank. If only I could make it to Woof. But the river between us seethes, dropping over submerged rocks and hissing when it comes back up.

Focusing my energy, I fight the currents that bully my body and twist my gown around my legs. Kicking, I try to get free of the cloth, but it only winds tighter and tighter in the whirling eddies. Wrapping my fingers around the slippery boulder, I take a deep breath and use all my strength to pull myself up. I need to get my tangled legs out of the water so that I can free them from the gown. Holding my breath and fighting the drag of the fierce current, I raise myself up several inches so that my head almost reaches the top of the boulder. Just a little farther and I can lean over the knobby rock.

A surge of water hits my back and swirls around my waist, sucking me down. In an instant, I lose the few inches I'd gained. Heart sinking with despair, I lean into the rock. I'll rest. Just for a minute. Just for a minute, I tell myself, shutting my eyes.

❊ ❊ ❊

I don't know how long I've been gripping this boulder. If seconds have passed or hours. But it's getting harder and harder to hold on. Both my arms scream with pain, and my teeth chatter from the cold. I can no longer hear Woof barking. And I am so tired.

Shifting one arm, I try to get a better grip on the slippery rock. My movements are clumsy, and the instrument in my pocket bangs against the boulder with a metallic clang. A bright blue beam erupts into the air.

The light undulates and dances on the water—as if alive—beckoning to me, asking me to follow. Am I hallucinating? My mind, sleepy with exhaustion, aches to give in.

But if I let go, I'll be sucked under.

And if I don't, I'll freeze to death.

A sapphire beam blazes across my boulder. *Refracted sunrays?* I marvel idly as my tired hands slide from the rock. My head goes under.

My first underwater breath burns through my lungs and snaps me to attention. *I refuse to drown!* Using my last strength, I kick harder and harder, finally freeing my legs from the gown. I fight my way back up to the surface. I take a quick, wheezing breath, but the river is too strong. My gown balloons up around me, and then it drops down, twisting back around my thighs. It drags me back under while I hold my last breath.

Blue light surrounds me. I float in it, watching translucent bubbles of color bob and dance. In the distance, I hear music. My body relaxes, letting go. I look down at the riverbed. A sapphire trail weaves its way through the rocks. I am drawn toward it.

A gush of force grabs me, tosses me, turns me, spins me in the frothy bubbles, and then spits me onto the bank. Coughing and vomiting silty water, I gasp for breath before collapsing on the rocky shore.

❋ ❋ ❋

I don't know how much time passes before I sit up weakly. I'm so thirsty that I cup my hands and scoop water out of the river, lapping it up like Woof.

After a while I've had my fill, but my stomach still rumbles unhappily. Candied carrots? No. My pack is gone and the map with it. Gulped down by the hungry river.

Then I remember. The flyers! I drag myself on all fours and hide in the shadow of a nearby outcropping of rock. Scanning the sky, I note that there isn't one in sight. Perhaps the river carried me past their range.

I exhale.

My legs wobble as I stand and shake the water out of my ears. I look all around but can't see any hint of the trail. I feel in my pocket and pull out the silver tube. The only thing I have left is this instrument. What did Melody call it? A flute? A lot of good it is going to do me.

I check the opposite bank. Woof is nowhere in sight. I must have been washed far down the river before making it across. It would probably take him days to get down here, considering the vertical cliffs on either side of the water...if he tries at all. And I hope he won't. It's too dangerous.

I can't stop trembling. I'm soaked. I place the flute on the ground near my feet and twist the cloth of my gown, wringing out water. I'm tempted to take if off and just leave it. This worthless white gown almost drowned me. But having left my traveling cloak by my pack, I don't have anything else to wear.

Tall rocks tower above me. Dark clouds billow overhead, matching my mood perfectly. It looks like rain. I need to keep moving.

A gust of wind blows across the lip of the flute, making a faint sound. A track of blue suddenly glows, catching my eye. It gleams on the ground like the slimy markings of a snail, only the color is the same blazing sapphire that surrounded me in the river.

The flute sounds a second time, softly.

Once again the blue light shimmers, curls, and seems to motion for me to follow. Hesitating, I glance at the roiling river, up at the sheer canyon walls, and then back at the bobbling blue light.

I have nothing to lose by following. Shoving the flute back into my chest pocket, I walk along the trail of the light. It leads me scrambling over boulders, around sandbars, and through strange plants that ooze a sticky juice. I carefully step over a mossy log and wish I had stepped more carefully before. I wouldn't have slipped and ended up over here, alone, without supplies, without the map.

As I climb higher into a dark crevice, I realize it's a good thing Woof isn't with me. He'd never be able to make this vertical climb. But I do miss him. His friendly company gave me support. I sigh and move with painstaking slowness now, hand over hand, carefully clinging to the steep crack between the sheer rock walls.

As I scale higher and higher, my stomach begins to knot with fear. I have never been so far off the ground before. I wonder if this is how Eris feels when she takes off into the sky. My feet fumble for holds, but I refuse to look down. Instead, I crane my head upward, straining toward the top of the cliff. I'm afraid, but I need to keep going. I need to get to the top. Grasping a stone with my right hand, I pull hard.

The rock comes off in my hand.

My feet flounder but find no grip.

Time seems to stop as my body falls away from the rock. The knot in my stomach leaps into my throat. I'm sliding straight down the cliff face!

"Help!" I whimper. But of course there is no one else to hear.

My hands claw the face of the rock, scrabbling for a hold. But nothing stops me until I land hard on my rear, hitting a narrow outcropping of rock. Panting, I stare at the sharp rocks below. *If it weren' t for this ledge....*

My whole body convulses. Needle pricks of fear shoot down my legs. I look back toward the cliff. The blue light continues to dance and beckon, flowing easily over the treacherous rock. Ignoring my sweating, bleeding hands, I gather my courage. There has to be another way.

But the rocks are even steeper elsewhere. When I tilt my

head back, I can see nothing but granite slab against granite sky. And I can't go back down. I survey the view. The murky water still rages below. The first splash of rain hits my nose. I need to get out of here, fast, before it really pours down and I won't be able to get a good grip.

Chewing my lip, I turn to face the rock. I brush the skinny beam of blue light with my finger. Is it warm? Or is that just my imagination? And, more importantly, where is it leading me?

It is starting to rain heavily now. The river will rise even higher. Soon there'll be a flood in this canyon. I force myself not to think. Just breathe and move. Breathe and move. I decide to move only one hand or foot at a time. If my feet had been firmly planted, I wouldn't have fallen. Right hand, left foot, left hand, right foot; I let go in order, keeping three limbs rooted as I laboriously make my way up the sheer cliff, ignoring the sharp pain in my left shoulder, the bruised ache in my back, and the gritty sting in my fingertips.

This time, the rock holds, and I pull myself over the treacherous stretch until I can once again climb comfortably. The air is heavy and moist, damp with storm and earthy scents rising up from the plants bordering the river. I shiver, my wet gown clinging to my back, and I continue up, up, following the thin blue line that snakes through the crevice.

At last I haul myself over the top.

Chapter 16

A CANTANKEROUS OLD MAN

BELOW ME STRETCHES a vast, green basin. Young trees sprinkle the land. Their leaves dance in the breeze and shimmer in the glints of sun that peek through the clouds. The meadow seems haphazardly cultivated. Stacked, tan-colored rocks form borders around agricultural plots that are placed in a patchwork around stone huts. The huts are also built in rock and topped with thatched roofs. They are squat and round and remind me of mushrooms.

A narrow animal track leads down from the ridge of the cliff. The rock face isn't nearly as steep on this side. Squinting, I try to see across the lowland, but the sheer cliffs on the other side of the basin seem to reflect the light in a violet haze. Hoisting myself over the last jagged edge, I take my first step down the path.

A sparkling rivulet meanders across the trail, and I suddenly realize how thirsty I am from the climbing. I can't believe I made it! Darin is the athletic one of the family. He would be amazed.

As I stoop to drink, I notice the polished green and topaz stones gleaming on the sandy stream bottom. Small blue flowers grow on the grassy banks. Jalene used to weave pictures like this into her storytelling, but she borrowed hers from geography cubes. Noveskina doesn't have any streams or rivers, just man-made canals.

Abruptly, a wave of grief weighs down on my chest. Tears prick my eyes, but I push my homesickness away. I will not think about Jalene. Or Aron. Or any of my friends. Not even Darin. Clenching my teeth, I stand straight and continue my course.

Before I know it, I reach the meadow. The day has already lost its morning freshness, and I can tell it is going to be warm. Taking in a deep breath, I smell the fragrance of spring flowers on the breeze.

Loud voices rise in the air, disturbing the tranquility of the natural scene. I glance around, trying to see who is making the noise, and spot two people standing in a narrow field between a couple of huts. They wave their arms vigorously. I take a few cautious steps closer to them and crouch behind a bush to watch. They're...*yelling*. I strain my ears, trying to hear why they are so upset.

"If your dog digs up my garden again, I'll...I'll...I'll...." Red sparks sizzle off the old woman's throat like the hot embers from a fire. One flies close to a dog cowering nearby. He yelps and runs away.

"You should talk, with that bedraggled creature you call a pet!" bellows the old man. A sickly green color flashes around his neck. The old man nudges a small feline animal away from him with his foot. The animal has fluffy white fur. Cat, I think, excitedly. It's a cat!

"How dare you!" shouts the woman. "Don't kick Chaz!"

The man points at the dog. "Well, don't bully Zuni!"

I've never seen adults behave like this before—like they are deranged. Backing up nervously, I wonder if a war is about to start.

The woman swoops in to pick up her cat. "I'd never hurt your dog. But I warn you, don't let your pet in the flower garden. Or I might come after you!" With head held high, the woman strides across a narrow field and disappears into one of the huts.

I shift from foot to foot, unable to decide whether or not to come out. Though I am curious about the people in this meadow, their yelling is dangerous. But I certainly can't go back the way I came.

I decide to walk as far around the two huts as I can so that the old man won't notice me. I hope that the other people who live here won't be so crazy or reckless. They might even speak with One Voice. But because the path I was following leads between the two huts, I'll have to find a different route. Maybe between those young trees—

"You, girl!" shouts the man, striding briskly toward me.

I jump. The man looks angry. And his face has something strange about it. The skin...it is wrinkled, toughened, furrowed...it's hideous and not at all like the smooth complexions of adult Noveskinians.

"Where did you come from?" he asks. His quick, black eyes look me up and down, taking in everything from my wrinkled gown to my rubber sandals.

I clear my throat and do my best to reply, wishing that I hadn't lost the map that Melody told me would serve as an introduction, "Um, I—"

"I've seen your garb before!" The old man interrupts, grabbing my wrist. "You must be Noveskinian." He turns and shouts, "Selma! Come out. Someone is here."

Flinching at the noise of his voice, I watch, terrified as the old woman emerges. She smoothes out her robe as she walks toward us. The fabric of her dress is rough and plain. It pales in comparison to the bright colors of Noveskinian gowns. And her skin is just as crinkled as the man's, although it is much darker—almost the color of the wooden cello. I bite my lip. What are they going to do to me?

"What is it, Rafe?" she asks the man while staring at me.

"This child has somehow made it here from Noveskina."

"Good grief." The woman wrings her hands. "Another spy?"

"I'm not a spy!" I protest. "I'm looking for—"

Rafe scowls at me. "Be quiet! We need to think." His grip is hard around my wrist, and I can't pull away. He turns to Selma and asks, "How would she have made it all the way over here? There is only one entrance on the far side. She would have been spotted before coming in this far."

Selma furrows her brows. "She could be a flyer. They've been sighted closer and closer. Rumor is the Masker's desperate for more farmers and servants."

"I'm not a flyer!" I protest. I twist and shake my arm, trying to free my wrist. "Let me go! I only wanted to find the Secret Valley."

Selma gives Rafe a worried look. "You see? She *is* looking for the Secret Valley. We have to bring her to the Council. Right away!"

Still gripping my arm, Rafe stoops down and picks up a bit of soil. He rubs it between his fingers. "I don't know. It's time to plant." He licks a bit of dirt off his palm. "This earth tastes ready for seeds. We can't waste time going to Council now—not with spring planting."

"You and your silly earth-licking," says Selma. "Don't you realize how important this is?"

"It's more important to get our seeds in now. Unless you don't care about eating?"

"We have time for both!" insists Selma. "It's only across the valley."

A pea green cloud looms over Rafe's head. "You know as well as I do that's half a day's walk each way."

Selma glares at him. "Selfish old man! We'll plant tomorrow. Or the next day! What difference does it make?" Red sparks kindle around her throat.

Zuni growls softly, and the cat appears, hissing and taking a swipe at the large, black dog.

"Keep your nasty cat away from my dog!" hollers Rafe.

Selma picks up Chaz and turns toward her hut. "Rafe, you are a cantankerous excuse for a man, but this time you have gone too far. The Council would never forgive us if we didn't warn them about a spy in our midst!"

"Cantankerous?" booms Rafe.

The strength of their voices scares me. It is unlike anything I've ever seen, more powerful than the relatively harmless shouts of ill-mannered children. I try to look brave, but I wonder if this is how the sound wars started—with people disagreeing and hurting each other with raised voices.

"If you had a scrap of sense," continues Rafe, "you'd realize that no one will be at the Council. Everyone will be as busy planting as we are. You're nothing but a stubborn old woman."

Selma spins around. "Stubborn?" she shrills, a hand on one hip. "When have I ever been stubborn? I didn't plant my blackberries next to your hut so they wouldn't take over. And I didn't build my path over your precious clay deposit, at no little inconvenience to myself, I might add. Now I have to walk twice as far to reach the stream." Her hand sweeps out in a wild, exaggerated gesture. "I even rearranged my marigold beds so they'd keep the bugs out of your lettuce!"

"Our lettuce," Rafe corrects. "Stubborn isn't the right word," he admits grudgingly. "But it's going to rain soon, and we need to plant before it does."

Selma looks at me and then at Rafe. "You're sure it's going to rain?"

Rafe nods. "If we want to eat next year, the seeds need to go in now."

Selma stares at me doubtfully. "I guess the Council won't be in session until after spring planting. Not many people will be available before then. And dealing with the spy should really be a community decision." She smiles as if they hadn't just participated in the worst fight I've ever seen.

"That's my lamb," says Rafe. I stare at the man, puzzled. A learning cube image of a fuzzy baby animal pops into my mind. The woman looks nothing like a lamb.

Selma smoothes the material of her skirt. "But what are we going to do with the child? How will we feed her?"

"I'm not a child!" I interrupt. "If I were home, I'd be Masked by now."

"Well then," says Selma, "exactly why aren't you home?"

Rafe ignores my outburst. "We'll ration our stores and watch her until the spring Council. Until then, she'll work. She will help us with the planting."

I want to cry with frustration. *Why did I lose Melody's map? It would have proved that I'm not a spy.* "Just let me go! You don't need to feed me. I'll leave. This is all a mistake. I told you that I was looking for the Secret Valley!"

The old man breaks into loud guffaws of laughter. The woman's eyes glisten with mirth. "This *is* the Secret Valley," she says.

"This? But it's out in the open. It's not secret at all."

The woman shrugs her bony shoulders. "It's secret enough," she says, giving me a meaningful look. "And it will stay that way."

I gather my courage and ask, "Can you at least let go of my wrist? I won't run away, and you're hurting me."

Rafe turns to Selma. "I can't hold her like this forever. Run into the house and get that relic we dug up the other day. I think we can use it."

Selma goes and returns with two rusty metal loops attached by a thick, metal chain.

"Put it around her ankles," says Rafe. "I think that contraption weighs enough to keep any flyer on the ground."

Selma bites her lip. "Seems cruel, to a child...."

"It won't hurt her," says Rafe. "And we can't have her flying off."

Selma twists the small key into each lock and opens the bands. She slips my ankles into the metal circles. When both loops are locked tight, Rafe lets go of my wrist. I take a step, and the heavy chain jangles as I move. "You don't have to do this!" I say. "I'm not a flyer! I'm not...anything."

Selma turns to me, her eyes widening with a glint of sympathy. "We are all something." She shakes her head. "If we're going to be working together, I suppose you should tell us your name."

"Miri," I answer, looking hopelessly at the empty fields that are to be my new prison. *Why did Melody send me here?* But, even as I ask the question, I know the answer: I had nowhere else to go.

Chapter 17

TILLING THE SOIL

RAFE RUBS HIS hands together. "We've wasted enough time. Let's get to work."

Selma shakes her head. "Miri looks exhausted. I'm going to let her rest and give her something to eat first."

Rafe looks as if he has something to say to that, but then he just shrugs. "Have it your way."

"I will," replies Selma, leading me into her hut. Chaz comes with us and curls in a shaft of sunlight that pours in through the window and illuminates beautifully woven blankets and tapestries that line the walls. As Selma tends to the hearth, I walk over to touch one of the wall hangings. Selma watches me. "It's my Talent," she says shortly.

"They're amazing," I whisper.

Next to the tapestries, baskets dangle from the rafters of the curved ceiling. The containers are all filled with food, mostly vegetables. One is heaped with potatoes. Another holds onions. The smallest basket is full of carrots. A soot-stained metal pot hangs on a hook over the fire. It looks as if it was banged together and welded out of many different pieces. They must scavenge metals from the old vehicles, too, I realize. The smell of boiled potatoes fills the air, making my stomach growl with hunger. It feels like years since the last time I had a warm meal.

Selma hands me a ceramic bowl with a ladle. "Serve yourself."

I scoop up a full bowl and tilt it back, drinking the thick soup. It is strangely spiced, pungent and warm like a hot summer day. "It's delicious," I say.

"My secret ingredients," says Selma with a small smile. "Curry and paprika."

As I drink, Selma unrolls a mat of woven grass and spreads it on the floor. She hands me one of her blankets. "Rest," she tells me brusquely as she leaves the hut. "You'll need it."

Too tired to argue, I stretch out under the blanket and close my eyes. It's hard to get comfortable. The metal rings around my ankles are cold against my skin. My shoulder is stiff and sore. And my legs throb where they were bashed against the boulder. The boulder that saved me, I remember, picturing Woof on the other bank of the river. I hope he made it home...wherever that is for him. My chest heaves. I don't have a home any more. Nothing but this strange, new life.

Even though I am exhausted, it seems I will never fall asleep. Everything is too unfamiliar. As I toss on the thin mat, something presses into my chest. I pull the flute out of my pocket and lay it beside me under the blanket. Finally, I doze off into a fitful sleep.

It seems only a few minutes have passed before Selma shakes me awake. "What's wrong?" I ask, noting the chilly, gray light of early morning.

"Nothing," replies Selma. "You slept an entire day and night. I'd let you sleep longer, but Rafe says you have to get up and work now."

I blink the sleep out of my eyes and blearily follow her to the hearth. Selma hands me a cup. It contains warm water infused with a strange golden herb that gives the drink a soft, mellow flavor. Selma passes me a cooked potato and says, "Best we go out now. Rafe'll be waiting." Straightening my rumpled gown, I follow her outside. Dawn birds twitter, and some robins hop about in the grass while I eat the plain potato.

Rafe meets us in the middle of the field, wearing a faded blue robe that only comes to his waist. Below, he has the strangest clothes I've ever seen—a gown that starts from his waist and separates into two separate casings, one for each leg. He holds out a shovel.

"Loosen and turn the soil," he commands, gesturing at the acres of earth stretching between, around, and behind his and Selma's dwellings.

Please, I think, grumpily, taking the shovel. I start digging into the packed dirt. It isn't as easy as I thought it'd be. The ground is hard, even frosty in the shady hollows, and I often have to stomp on the shovel to get it to go in. The chain between my legs slows my every move and reminds me that I am as much a prisoner here as I was in the Masker's house. Selma and Rafe work close beside me. Every once in a while they throw me wary looks as we break the clods up into soft earth. We work silently for the entire morning.

I feel the grit on my face as I wipe the sweat from my forehead with the back of my hand. The sun is high and hot now, and my mouth is parched with thirst. My shoulders hurt, the small of my back aches, and blisters puff up on my fingers. Clumsily, I wrap my hands in the sleeves of my gown, knowing there is no point in complaining. I watch the two adults for a moment, wondering if they will ever quit.

Selma and Rafe look older than most elders in Noveskina— the skin on their faces is so creased—but Rafe doesn't even appear tired. He is actually whistling, like a bird, a merry tune as if he is enjoying himself! Even the color of his song reflects his cheerful mood—today the green around his throat is the color of fresh spring shoots.

Every once in a while, Rafe stops whistling and Selma sings where he leaves off. It shocks me to hear an adult singing so freely, but it also sounds pretty. A small hum begins at the back of my throat.

Selma stops abruptly. "We take turns singing, Miri."

The hum dies in my throat. "Why?"

"It's too dangerous to sing together. It could damage the crops and wreak all sorts of havoc if we were out of tune."

I nod as if I understand, but really I don't. We go back to work, and my life slips into a monotony of bending, stomping, and lifting until Selma says, "Time to eat."

I sink beside Selma and Rafe under the pine saplings that border the field and take the boiled egg and goat cheese Selma offers. Rafe passes around an animal skin bag filled with water, and we take turns squirting the liquid into our mouths.

I stretch my sore arms. "Are we going to rest this afternoon?"

Rafe snorts. "Rest!" he repeats, incredulously. "We've hardly begun. There are irrigation ditches to be dug and—"

"Miri should rest," interjects Selma. "She's a child, and she isn't used to working like this."

"She's already rested. She slept a whole day and night, for land's sake! She's young. She can work," insists Rafe.

"Tomorrow," Selma says firmly.

Rafe raises his voice and the color around his throat thickens to a pea green. "Selma, you bossy, old cat, Miri works if she wants to eat! That's final."

"Fine," says Selma, pulling me up with her strong grip. "But she'll tend the animals this afternoon. Look at her hands!

She's had enough digging for one day."

"You are one stubborn old woman," Rafe laughs.

Selma ignores him. She speaks rapidly as we walk, explaining what she wants done. Her instructions are foreign, and the weight of the chains shortens my steps and distracts me from her words. We come to a small wooden building, and she flings the door open. Instantly there is a commotion of flapping, crowing chaos.

"Wh—what do you want me to do?"

"I just told you!" she replies, exasperated. "You *can* milk a goat and feed a few chickens, can't you?" she asks, handing me a small basket. I nod, too embarrassed to admit that I've only ever seen the likeness of these animals in my learning cubes.

"Don't forget to look under the roosts for any eggs I missed," Selma adds, handing me a basket. "And never mind the rooster. Then go around to the other side of the shed and milk the goat. You'll find a bucket close by." She smiles. "When you're all through with that, you can sneak in for a wee rest, Miri. Rafe'll never be the wiser."

This shouldn't be too hard, I tell myself, watching Selma hurry back to her work. Farmers outside the Wall do this all the time. As I walk inside the pen, the birds fluff their feathers and cackle suspiciously. Taking a deep breath, I reach my hand gingerly under the first chicken's straw roost. There are lots of droppings but no egg. The bird digs her beak into my hand. "Ouch!"

I slip my hand more cautiously under the next perch. This chicken doesn't seem too disturbed, so I grab the warm egg and move on. The third chicken doesn't even wait for me to feel for an egg. Instead, she flaps her wings furiously and pecks my wrist in a flurry of angry feathers.

Taking a hasty step back, I slip in the chicken goo that coats the earth floor and tumble backwards—straight into the muck. My basket lands on top of me, breaking the one egg onto my face. Sitting up, I wipe the yolk and shells out of my eyes.

The rooster crows, his red comb wobbling with apparent delight.

"Go away, you ratty bird!" I call, thoroughly annoyed with his self-satisfied strutting.

"Er-er-er-er-errr!" he replies.

My gown is repulsive—covered with stinky chicken droppings. I snort with disgust, stand, and grab my basket, determined to get the rest of the eggs, no matter what.

None of the other chickens seems to mind my presence. I probably smell just like them. I gather the last two eggs and walk around the shed feeling a little bit better about myself.

My confidence doesn't last long. In greeting, the goat butts her head against my belly, tumbling me to the ground and nearly breaking the eggs in my basket. "You stupid, unTalented goat!"

The goat looks innocently at me, batting her long lashes.

"Hold still!" I rack my brain and recall a learning cube lesson about farmers milking cows. How much harder can it be? I grab a rough wooden stool and an old metal bucket and place them near the animal. Then I reach under the goat for one of her udders and squeeze. No milk. I squeeze again, telling myself to be patient.

The goat takes a few steps away.

I move my stool closer and begin again. After a while, I start to get the hang of it. Rhythmically, I pull and squeeze one teat with my right hand and then the other with my left. The bucket fills with a steady stream of milk. "That's right," I say.

"This isn't so bad, is it?"

As if in answer to my question, the animal steps back and to the side, knocking over my bucket.

"Noise and damnation!"

Rafe and Zuni round the corner. "Having problems?" Rafe asks.

"Nothing I can't deal with," I lie.

Rafe raises his eyebrows. "Good." He puts the shovel away and leaves. I squeeze the goat's teat a little while longer, but there isn't much milk left. The brief stillness of evening descends—that twilight time when the day creatures hush and the night ones have not yet begun to sound. I've missed my chance to nap, plus I don't have much milk to show for my efforts—and only two eggs. My gown is a mess, and I hate this work. My back hurts, my ankles throb, my wrist is bleeding from the pecking chicken, and I'll never get the dirt out from under my fingernails. It's worse than being a house servant. If only I could escape—but where to? I sigh and head back to the hut.

Chapter 18

PRACTICE

DAY AFTER DAY, I work turning the soil until my muscles scream with pain. Rafe has no sympathy when I ask for a break. "We can't afford to support a beggar. You'll work until we take you to Council. They'll decide what to do with you then."

"Could you at least take these cuffs off?" I bend down and slide the metal bands up on my leg, showing him a raw, red welt that stripes my ankle. In places, it oozes.

Rafe shakes his head. "We can't take the risk."

Selma winces. "That looks painful. I'll run in and get my salve. It will help the skin to heal."

As she makes her way back to the hut, Rafe returns to tilling the soil, motioning for me to follow behind and rake out the clods. He must not have a heart, I think. The wound around my ankle burns hotly, and I'm so busy glaring at Rafe's back that I don't notice Selma reappear.

"Look what I found," she says. Rafe and I turn. She is holding my silver flute. "I dropped the salve onto your mat by accident. And when I went to pick it up, I felt something hard." Selma stares at me. "Where did you get this, Miri?"

"You took it from Secret Valley folk, didn't you?" accuses Rafe.

"No!" I cry. "I would have shown it to you, but you wouldn't listen to my story. I was afraid you wouldn't believe me."

"We're listening now," Rafe says grimly.

I speak so fast that I'm almost babbling as I tell them of my journey through the deadlands, my escape from the flyer, and my brush with drowning in the river. My mouth is parched and dry. It feels like I've been talking for hours, but the sun has barely moved in the sky.

Selma puts her rough palm under my chin and tilts my head up so that I'm looking right into her eyes. "How did you make it here from the river?"

I point back, toward the ridge. "I climbed over those rocks."

"She's lying!" says Rafe. "Those rocks are impassable."

"Unless..." Selma's word trails off.

"How did you climb them?" Rafe barks his question at me.

I tell the truth, as crazy as it sounds. "There was a blue light that showed the way. I saw it first in the river. It seemed to lead me."

Selma claps her hands together. "The ley lines. Miri saw the ley lines! Rafe, do you know what this means?"

"No one has been able to see them since Patrice," Rafe says slowly.

"What are ley lines?" I ask, confused.

Selma's crooked teeth flash in a smile. "I've never seen them, but ley lines are crystallized sound patterns embedded in the earth. Patrice called them the song of the land."

I scratch my ankle. "Who was Patrice?"

"Patrice was our leader," says Selma. "The founders of the Secret Valley came from many different cities, but they joined together because they wanted nothing to do with the sound wars. More than a hundred years ago, Patrice led these people to this sound-protected valley by following the ley lines."

"And no one outside the Secret Valley knows about them," says Rafe as he pulls a key from his pocket. Bending down, he fits it into the keyholes on my cuffs and unlocks them. "You're no spy."

Selma kneels and gently applies a thick salve to the oozing sores on my ankles. "I'm so sorry we had to keep you in chains, Miri. Things will be better from now on."

"Except for one thing," says Rafe, shielding his eyes as he gazes at the cloudless sky. "Those flyers might still be looking for you. The Council might not let you stay if they think you'll bring the Masker upon us."

I swallow hard. "Surely the Council won't make me return to Noveskina!"

Selma shakes her head. "They can't do that, but they might send you back into the wild."

"To die," I whisper. There's no way I could survive in the wilderness alone. "Couldn't you just keep me here?" I ask Selma. "Nobody ever seems to come around."

Selma's forehead furrows into a million wrinkles. "I'm sorry, Miri. Even if we could hide you, we don't grow enough food in this clay-filled soil to feed three people."

Rafe waves a wasp away from his face. "It might help if Miri played that wind instrument. At least it would convince them that she's not a Noveskinian spy."

"The Council could use another wind instrument," adds Selma, handing me the flute. "They might be willing to risk keeping you for that."

I turn the instrument back and forth in my hands. "I don't know how to play it."

"You'll have to learn," says Rafe. "Before the Council

meets. Give it a try."

I hold the instrument up to my mouth and try to recall Melody's gestures. I blow through one end and then the other. The only sound that comes out is that of my breath hitting metal. I purse my lips inside the hole, pucker them around the outside of it, and tap the keys. But no sound comes out of the flute. "This thing is as ornery as the stupid goat!" I groan.

Rafe looks at me. "I reckon that's your fault and not the instrument's. You'll have to keep trying."

I let out a disgusted breath. A strange sound, like the low moan that comes from blowing over a bottle top, wavers in the air. "Listen!" I exclaim, and I make the sound over and over again.

Selma gives me a big smile, but Rafe only picks up his hoe. "You can practice more tonight. We'd better get back to work or we won't get the plants in before the Council meets."

The weeks pass and the days grow longer. Despite my growing anxiety about the upcoming Council meeting, I realize I'm beginning to enjoy working with the earth. My muscles have become taut and strong and my skin golden. Tender shoots sprout out of the soil. Rafe points out the lettuce shoots and tells me that they always come up first. I watch the plants eagerly, impatient for harvest. I am so sick of potatoes that I never want to eat another one as long as I live.

And there is a new camaraderie between the three of us as we work. Rafe and Selma take turns singing all sorts of tunes. Some are so pretty that I wish I could share them with Jalene. But even if I returned home, there is no singing in Noveskina.

Selma encourages me to take a turn. At first, my voice

is rusty and hoarse, but after a while I get used to making the unfamiliar sounds and notice how much faster it makes the work go.

"Your voice is still too timid," grumbles Rafe.

I think my voice is quite strong, but I don't bother to object. I know now that Rafe is mostly bluster and no real harm. He even does the dishes by himself at nights, insisting that I practice the flute.

Night after night, I work with the instrument. Eventually, I discover that pressing down on the keys makes different sounds. I can play about six notes perfectly, so I run through them over and over again.

After over an hour of practice, Rafe stops me and says with a strained smile, "That's enough for tonight, Miri." Relieved, I join him in his corner.

At first I thought Rafe's Talent was tapping out rhythms on his hand drums, but he explains that it isn't a soul gift. His music comes through hard practice. Rafe's Talent is working with clay. Some nights, he teaches me how to spin the clay around the wheel that I keep going with a foot pump.

"That's fine," says Rafe.

Watching my ball of clay begin to take shape, I ask, "Do you think this could be my Talent?"

Rafe points at my hands. "You tell me."

I look down at the thick, lumpy shape and shake my head.

"Not that you couldn't get good with plenty of practice," he observes, running his hands through his thinning hair. "But I don't think it's a deep soul gift if that's what you mean. You'd have to work hard at it."

"I wouldn't mind working at most things," I complain, "if I had one single Talent that came naturally to me, like you and

Selma and all my friends."

Rafe gazes at me seriously. "I'd give the subject a rest if I were you. Trying too hard can push things away, you know. It's like the seeds we planted. If I kept digging them up to see if they were growing, then they never would grow."

"But I *had* to think about finding my Talent in Noveskina. That's practically all we do once we turn ten—find, explore, and develop our Talents." My head droops. "Only I never found mine."

"My point exactly," says Rafe. "You never had a chance to give it a rest. It's terrible hard on late bloomers." He rubs a lump in the clay I am turning. "Still, you're here now. Relax and see what happens."

My hands loosen up, and I feel the clay spinning round and round against them. Maybe Rafe is right. Maybe if I quit trying so hard to find my Talent, one will have a chance to grow, just like the seeds.

I stop the wheel. Rafe looks at my creation. "Not bad," he says. "Not bad at all. This one almost looks like a bowl. You're getting better. If you're around long enough, I'll show you how to glaze the pots."

If I'm around long enough. I clamp the thought down, trying not to visualize myself in exile. Or worse, brought back to Noveskina by the flyers. Pushing my fears out of my mind, I stand to give Rafe back his seat.

As I straighten my gown over my legs, I notice the material is stained despite being freshly washed the day before. Splotches of color shimmer in the folds and creases: green grass stains, black streaks of dirt, brownish spots of blood, purple....

I stare at the purple. *Where did it come from? And the*

pink, yellow, blue, orange, and fuchsia? Little dots of color hide along the sleeves and hem of the fabric. I bite my lip, thinking hard. What could the material be reacting to?

Selma interrupts my thoughts from across the room, "Tomorrow is the day."

I look up. "Are we going to harvest the lettuce?"

"No," answers Selma. "Tomorrow the Council meets."

Chapter 19

THE COUNCIL

I TOSS AND turn all night, unable to sleep. The following morning, we leave so early that I can still see the last stars. The early dawn blooms into such a profusion of apricot and gold that I wonder if my night fears were perhaps unfounded. The beautiful day seems to promise that everything will be well.

First we pass across Selma and Rafe's fields, trailed by Zuni. Chaz rides along in Selma's basket. Filigrees of green leaf and bud, stalk, and root lace the loamy soil. Even though I'm full of dread, I feel proud of the small plants, as if I am personally responsible for their growth. We walk by the neighboring huts where the earth also smells fresh and tilled.

All sorts of people join us on the road, from skipping children to stooped old men. They are bright and colorful in their patchwork clothes, and I'm thrilled to be meeting people other than Rafe and Selma. I hope to even meet someone my own age. But folks give me stabbing, suspicious looks. One dark-haired woman stares, her eyes narrowing angrily. "Where did this stranger come from?"

Selma puts a protective arm around me. "You'll hear about that at Council, Matilda."

The woman nods her head sharply, but her expression does not soften.

Many people carry objects of various shapes and sizes wrapped in blankets. Although I am curious about the bundles, I don't want to draw more notice to myself by asking what they are. The group walks silently across the wakening earth. People glance warily at me from the corners of their eyes.

"Ignore them," whispers Rafe. "Just think about the beautiful day and the warm sun on your shoulders."

I follow Rafe's advice and watch the dogs and cats leading the crowd. Someone even brought her goat. It's too bad Nonce can't see this—a whole community where people have relationships with animals! I wish Woof were still with me. He'd protect me from whatever lies ahead.

The young girl at the front of the group breaks my unpleasant train of thought by piping up in song, "When the sun shines in the morning."

"You've just got to get up!" sings an old woman in reply.

Soon everyone takes turns, adding in phrases about our daily tasks: feeding the chickens, tilling the soil, planting the seeds, baking the bread, milking the goat. There isn't a single one of these chores that I haven't tried, I realize somewhat proudly. I hum under my breath as the level trail unwinds beneath my feet. Selma nudges my shoulder. "Only one person sings at a time."

The trail gradually widens into a dirt road. A breeze blows, shaking the pearly blossoms from the fruit trees and mantling the earth with fluffy white. I sniff, and for a moment, the soft fragrance lets me forget my troubles.

But when we enter the heart of the Secret Valley, I can't keep my fear down any longer. My knees go weak as we pass stone cottages sitting side by side in a square around an inner courtyard. There is a stone fountain at the center, spraying water from the long nose of a pirouetting animal. To distract myself, I think back to my learning cubes and try to place the creature. A fellytant. No, that's not right. An elephant.

A man standing by the fountain turns to face me. He stares at my clothing.

Selma stares back. She drapes her blanket around my shoulders, covering my gown, and takes a seat. I sit down alongside her and huddle beneath the blanket even though the day is warm. "I still don't understand why this valley is considered secret," I whisper to Selma. "Everything is out in the open."

Selma places Chaz on her lap and strokes the cat's long fur. "Everything seems open, but the valley is wedged between the cliffs and river on one side and the mountains on the other. It's nearly impenetrable and protects us. That's why people were able to survive here during the sound wars."

Like Noveskina's sound Wall, I think.

"Shh!" admonishes Rafe. "We're beginning."

One by one, people reach under their blankets. With elaborate care, they begin to unveil musical instruments. My jaw drops. They have so many! Most of the instruments are fairly simple and made of wood. Some have fine, animal gut strings. I see a few drums made out of clay and covered tautly with hides. There are clarinets, violins, cymbals, and a few other instruments I don't recognize. The Masker said he had the only instruments left—that the others had all been destroyed. Where did these instruments come from?

Rafe taps a steady beat on his drum. Around him, the air vibrates a brilliant lime. He stops, and a wooden clarinet takes up a refrain. The burgundy color from the clarinet is still hanging in the air when a violin fills the sky with indigo.

Lavender tendrils of harp take up where the violin leaves off. Colors swirl in the air, and my hands flutter with some crazy desire to shape them. It is so easy to imagine how the different strands of music might be woven together like Selma's blankets to make a beautiful pattern.

A pretty girl in a quilted tunic begins to sway to the guitar, interpreting the music gracefully with her nimble body. Selma stands and says to Rafe, "Watch Miri. I'm going to dance!" She moves next to the young woman, twirling freely, her homespun skirt whirling brightly. I long to join them, but I haven't the faintest idea of how to begin. I've never seen people move like this before, tapping their feet to the rhythms, swaying with the melodies. Besides, I can't make myself conspicuous.

The colors in the air become so bright that it hurts to look, like staring at the sun. I close my eyes and lose myself in the dizzy joy of the music. When I open them again, colors wash over me. The children have halos of blue, green, and yellow flickering around them. Some of the older people are enveloped in a sunny golden haze. The women holding children are suffused with pink light. Everything is so beautiful that I relax. Abruptly, the cymbals cut off in mid-sentence.

"We are ready," announces a tall man.

Selma and the other dancers take their seats.

"Are there any requests for energy?"

A woman stands and says she needs help with her fruit trees. They are late in blossoming. "Let's see what I can do. Help me direct it," the man tells the crowd. He chants a deep note. The crowd stares at the fountain, brows furrowed in concentration. Earthy browns and soft shell pinks form a colorful ball above the elephant. I see something take shape— a slender tree topped with rosy blossoms. The man deepens his voice, and the sound image soars southward. Selma turns to me to explain. "This would be more powerful if we could sing and play our instruments together. But without a conductor our noises clash dangerously, so this is the safest way to share the Council's energy. We all help to focus the sound."

A mother stands. "My baby is feverish."

Another woman stands and sings a long, deep note. Again, the people focus their attention on the fountain. A bubble of pink enfolds the baby, cradling her in soft colors.

The Council meets several other requests, sending focused beams of energy to anyone in need. Then the tall man asks, "Do we have any business to discuss?"

People talk about how to rotate their crops, what to use for fertilizer. Someone's goat is sneaking into someone else's pasture. A separating couple argues over the division of possessions. I listen, trying to distance myself from my anxiety. As the Council business seems to go on forever, I become hopeful. Maybe I'm not that important after all. Maybe the Council won't even have time to discuss me.

Then Rafe stands. "I would like to introduce a guest."

I jerk back to attention.

Rafe gently pulls me up. "This is Miri."

My smile feels like a grimace frozen across my face.

"Why is she wearing a Noveskinian gown?" asks the man who had stared at me earlier.

"Yes!" exclaims a fierce-looking older woman with rheumy red eyes. "What's she doing here? We don't want any Noveskinians!"

I flinch.

Rafe raises his voice. "Miri ran away from Noveskina because she didn't want to be Masked."

"How do you know she's not a spy?" asks the woman, glowering at me.

"Because," says Rafe, "she followed the ley lines to get here!"

The crowd begins to murmur. "Nonsense!" cries the old woman. "She couldn't have followed the ley lines! They only responded to Patrice."

"If she didn't follow the ley lines," yells Selma, "how do you think she made it to our side of the valley without one of you seeing her?"

"She's a flyer!" shouts the rheumy-eyed woman. A sharp, black hiss erupts from the crowd. "A flyer has found our valley!"

Faces turn toward me, eyes blazing like sharp knives. "Are there others?" asks a young woman.

"No," replies a man. "We've posted lookouts. We would have seen them."

"Then how did this one get in?"

The discussion blasts around me like a turbulent wave. Muddied colors cloud around people's throats. "Send her away!"

"We can' t. She'd fly back to Noveskina!"

"Keep her prisoner."

"To die like the other one!"

The arguing grows louder and more ferocious. Birds squawk. Several cats arch their backs and hiss. The dogs around me work themselves into a frenzy, their fangs dripping saliva, as they bark and bark. I steel myself, hoping these people can control their animals.

Chapter 20

LUDA

AS THE NOISE grows, Rafe steps between me and the crowd. "Play your flute, Miri! Now!"

I pull the flute from the inner pocket of my gown. My hands shake so badly that I can barely hold the instrument. I lift it to my lips and blow lightly across the hole. A breathy note trembles in the air.

The dogs stop barking and they perk their ears.

I blow again, playing for my life.

The crowd quiets. Heads turn toward me.

The whiskered old woman puts her gnarled hand out covetously. "We don't have one of those yet. Where did you get that?"

Instead of answering, I vary the six notes I know into a simple melody.

People nod their heads. "Not bad," says the old lady, her voice carrying over the crowd. "This is no spy. Noveskinians don't even know these instruments still exist. And they sure can't play them."

As I continue to play, lulling the people and their animals, the tall man steps forward. "The Council could use that instrument—is it a flute? Perhaps you could tell us where you got it, Mara."

I stop playing, but I am too nervous to correct him on my name. "From the Masker's instruments."

People don't look too surprised at my news. The man continues his interrogation. "Why did you take it? Did you know we needed instruments?"

"No," I answer honestly.

"And how did you really find our valley?" asks the man.

The crowd is absolutely quiet, a sea of eyes gazes at me, waiting for my story. I decide to begin with the ley lines. Rafe and Selma seemed most impressed when they found out I could see them. "I didn't want to be Masked, so I ran away. I fell in the river on the other side of the valley. I thought I was going to drown, but a blue line of light showed me the way out of the river. When I got out, I saw the light continued. It stretched over the cliffs. I was lost and I didn't know what else to do, so I followed it. The light led straight to Rafe and Selma's huts."

At first, no one reacts to my story. I open my mouth thinking it might have been better to mention Melody's map, even if I no longer have it.

Before I have a chance to say anything, the tall man speaks, "I don't think she's lying. It's improbable that she's a flyer. Our lookouts would have spotted a flyer entering this valley from any direction." He turns to the people. "What do you say? Should we welcome Mara to the Secret Valley?"

"Miri," I say softly.

The crowd roars approval. Again, voices begin speaking at once. "We could use another young worker."

"She can stay with me!"

"I need the help, with my man gone."

"I need her," growls the old man behind me. "My rheumatism...."

I tug on Rafe's sleeve. "Can't I stay with you?"

Rafe shakes his head. "I'm sorry, Miri. We'd love to keep you. But our lands can't support an extra person."

Suddenly, a low amber note blows out across the crowd. The people fall quiet.

"I do not call your attention with the power of this oboe lightly," says a small woman. Her skin is almost as smooth as an adult Noveskinian's, but the silver streaks in her brown hair tell her age. The cockatiel on her shoulder chirps as the people stare at the woman expectantly.

"As you all know," continues the woman, "my daughter has been doing us a service in Noveskina. We would not have half of these instruments without her. I think it only fair that this young woman stay and help me until Melody returns."

Melody! My mind races. Melody is *from* the Secret Valley?

"Luda speaks true," says Selma. "I should have thought of it myself. She is the best one to help Miri adjust to our ways."

People clap and cheer. The colors around their throats grow bright and clear, and they settle back to business as if they hadn't just been shouting like a bunch of lunatics. A woman relays some news about traders. A man speaks of an irrigation project. A child asks if schooling can begin again now that planting is finished.

At last, the Council meeting ends, and people break up into informal groups, unpacking picnics from baskets and sharing what they have. Rafe and Selma bring me to Luda to make the formal introductions.

"She's a good worker and not much bother," says Rafe gruffly. "Just don't let her near your animals." Selma laughs and recounts my disastrous attempt to collect chicken eggs.

Luda's hazel-gold eyes twinkle. "It'll be a help to have her."

She spreads a blanket on the ground, inviting us to sit, and sets down a basket of dried cherries. Selma brings out a loaf of bread and some cheese.

Rafe pops a handful of cherries into his mouth. "Tell the truth, I'm going to miss Miri."

"Luda needs the help," Selma admits, putting her arm around me. "But I'll miss you, too."

I smile at Rafe and hug Selma. "Thank you for everything," I say. Then I turn to Luda. "You know, I met Melody."

Luda leans toward me. "You know my daughter? How?"

"I was forced to stay with the Masker for a while."

Luda smiles eagerly. "You'll have to tell me all about it. How is she?"

I don't answer. How can I tell Luda how wan and starved her daughter looked?

Rafe takes another handful of cherries and stands. "We'd best be off if we're to make it home before dark."

Luda stands, too. "And we have as far to go in the other direction."

Rafe tousles my hair. "See you when the Council meets this summer. Been my pleasure to have you 'round. Come on, Selma," he says thickly.

Selma cups my chin with her wrinkled palm. "You come visit us any time, understand? You're always welcome, lamb."

"Thank you. Goodbye!" I swallow around the lump growing in my throat and watch them walk away. I wave until they round the corner out of the square.

Luda picks up her oboe and wraps it carefully in a worn shawl. "We'd better go, too, Miri." The yellow and gray cockatiel rides comfortably on her shoulder, as well trained as a Noveskinian songbird.

I follow her down the street and back into the valley. This time, we head up a rutted dirt road that climbs toward the purple hills. A question nags at the back of my mind like a sore tooth, and I finally ask, "Did the Secret Valley folk...kill the spy?"

Luda sighs. "No. At least, not intentionally. It might have been the hard work she wasn't used to. Or perhaps the guilt she felt for being caught. Folks felt bad, but we couldn't have let her return to Noveskina to report to the Masker. Luda shudders. "We'd all have become servants then."

"I can understand people not wanting to be Masked as Noveskinian servants or farmers," I say, following Luda past a farm with a cherry orchard. "Especially when they can farm here for themselves."

Luda's bird flutters off her shoulder and darts between blossoming branches. "Secret Valley folks hate all Masks, not just the ones for servants."

"But, why?"

"You'd understand if you knew anything about the history of the Masks," answers Luda.

"I do know their history," I insist, stepping over a mud hole. "They were invented to save Noveskina during the sound wars. They gave us unity. And now they help people use their voices safely."

Luda's lip curls derisively. A flicker of earthy-brown shimmers around her. "Is that what you think?"

"Yes, it is," I reply somewhat defensively. "Everyone wears Masks in Noveskina, and it hasn't done us any harm." The boards of the worn bridge groan as we cross over the silvery creek. "Even your daughter is Masked."

Luda shakes her head. "I suppose there's no harm in telling

139

you this now that you are here to stay: Melody only pretends to be Masked. That is how she uses her Talent."

I stop walking. "She can pretend that? And the Masker doesn't notice?"

Luda doesn't answer right away. We see a fish leap up out of the creek water. Its scales shine in the evening light before it splashes back down. "Melody has the Talent of camouflage—of appearing to be what she is not. I pray that the Masker doesn't find out," she adds grimly. Then she shrugs, "As long as Melody can hum, I'm sure she'll be fine."

"*That's* why she was always humming when the Masker was around!" I exclaim.

Luda looks at me sharply. "You heard her?"

"Of course."

She frowns. "Did the Masker?"

"He didn't seem to notice. That was one of the things that puzzled me."

Luda's face clears. "Well, that's a relief. But I wonder why you can hear it. And why you can see the ley lines."

I scramble after Luda over the boulder-strewn trail. "I don't know, but I wonder why Melody stays in Noveskina if it's so dangerous."

"There are many reasons," says Luda, pausing at a stone outcropping. "But, most importantly, we need her there. She brings instruments to the valley and teaches us how to play them. You can't imagine how much help it is to have them." She smiles at me. "Now I hope you'll answer some of my questions."

I nod, looking over the valley.

"How did you get out of Noveskina?"

We watch the sun turn into a red orb, casting fiery fingers over the land, while I share my whole story. Luda flinches when

I describe the way the Masks sizzled as they sealed onto my friends' faces, and she looks even grimmer when I explain how I was caught. The sun sinks below the horizon as I tell her that I would never have escaped if Melody had not helped me.

Luda's face blanches. "Melody helped you escape?"

"She was wonderful! She gave me the flute—"

Luda taps her fingers on the rock. Abruptly, she stands. "Let's go. I don't want to get caught out here in the dark, and I have to...."

Luda doesn't finish her sentence. She practically flies down a path of smooth round stones and flings open the door to her hut.

As soon as we are inside, Luda hastily kindles a fire in the decoratively painted hearth. Looking around the cozy room, I nervously admire the neat lace tablecloth, the fluttering print curtains, the scrubbed wooden table, and the colorful paintings on the walls.

"Make yourself comfortable, Miri." Luda motions to a pad on the floor. "I need a minute." She seems so distracted and preoccupied that I don't dare ask why.

Sitting on the pad, I watch as Luda's features become curiously blank and absent. It looks like she is in some sort of trance. Her eyes are vague, and she stands completely still. There is something familiar about her expression. When she cocks her head to one side, I know.

I remember that Ceiron once looked at me in exactly that way, listening to my thoughts. I remember, too, the way he looked as if he'd been slapped when he heard my resentment at his intrusion.

"Y—you're a listener?" I was used to Ceiron's Talent, but I'm embarrassed to be so exposed to this stranger.

Luda blinks. It takes a second for her eyes to focus. "Yes—but please try not to interrupt—you must know how important concentration is to a listener."

"I–I'm sorry...."

She rubs her eyes. "It's no use anyway." Then her kind gaze rests on me. "You needn't look so bashful. I wasn't trying to listen to you. We don't use listeners to pry into people's minds here."

"We don't use listeners that way in Noveskina either!"

A look of such revulsion flits across her face that I back up a few steps.

"Stop," cautions Luda.

I turn, figuring I must have rubbed against one of her paintings. Instead, I see the lank skin of a face—a dead face—tacked up on the wall.

Chapter 21

A TALENT

I JUMP AWAY. "What is it?"

"My Mask," Luda replies.

I can't believe what I am hearing. "That's your Mask, and you took it *off?*"

"I didn't exactly take it off—it came off on its own. They do, if a person believes in something so strongly that she manages to raise her voice despite wearing one." Luda plunks herself on the braided, rag rug and begins chopping onions on a wooden plank as if having a dead Mask leering at us from the wall is no big deal.

I can't take my eyes off the hideous thing. There are seams where it has been carefully patched and stitched together. "I didn't think they Masked people in the Secret Valley."

"They don't," Luda says matter-of-factly. "Before my Mask came off, I lived in Noveskina. I keep it to remind myself, when the work is hard and the food scarce, of exactly why I don't wish to return to the Walled City."

"How come you left in the first place? Were they going to make you a house servant, too?"

"No, they wouldn't have made me a servant." Luda smiles wryly, holding out a peeler.

Taking it, I absently peel a carrot. "Then what happened?

Why did you take it off?"

Luda scrapes the edge of her finger with the knife. "Ouch!"

The bird on her shoulder shrills as Luda sucks the bleeding cut. Finally, she speaks. "That's something I don't like to think of, much less talk about."

I finish peeling my carrot in the uncomfortable silence that settles around us, my mind awhirl with questions that Luda will not answer.

"I'm sorry if I seem rude. I'm just so worried about Melody. I miss her so much. I even miss her mangy dog. And lately I haven't even been able to hear her—"

I can't help interrupting. "You can hear her from here?"

"Distance doesn't matter to an unMasked listener," answers Luda. "Our Talent develops further, but I can't hear Melody when she's humming to block out the Masker. Then, all I get is static." Luda's cheek twitches. "This past month, it has been nothing but static—as if she were humming all the time. That's why I was so worried when you told me she'd helped you to escape…. What if the Masker caught her?"

"I'm sure she's okay." I try to comfort Luda, but there is a hollow feeling in the pit of my stomach. If she isn't, then it is partly my fault for selfishly involving her in my problems.

"Yes, you're probably right," says Luda, but there is a worried line between her eyebrows, and she doesn't sound convinced. She picks up a potato.

I try to think of something that will relieve her anxiety. "Melody told me the Masker would never suspect her. She had an excuse for my disappearance. She planned to tell the Masker that his life partner had returned and helped me escape."

Luda gives a pleased laugh. "Brilliant! Melody *is* a quick thinker." Luda chops the potato vigorously. "Now let's talk

144

about something else." She pauses for a second and then asks a little too brightly, "Did you enjoy the Council music?"

"Yes. I loved the way colors shot out of the instruments when people played," I say enthusiastically. "And then everyone's individual colors became so bright. Brighter than anything I've ever seen."

Luda stops chopping. "What colors?"

"You know. The colors that happen when people sing, or play the instruments, or," I grin, "shout."

"No," she answers slowly. "I've never seen them."

I'm stunned and don't know what to say. *Is she blind to the colors?* Luda's hazel eyes are so sharp and penetrating that they look almost flinty. "Are those the only times you see colors?"

"No. I see them when the birds sing. I saw them when Rafe and Selma argued and when my friends were Masked. You remember how I told you I wasn't allowed to be Masked? And so I sneaked in to watch?" I continue for some reason, really wanting to explain everything and for Luda to understand. "Well, I wasn't allowed to be Masked because..." I pause. I hate talking about this, but it is the one thing I haven't already shared: "I don't have a Talent."

Luda lets out a deep periwinkle belly laugh. "Now, that's a joke! You don't have a Talent. My eye." She points at my gown. "That's a Noveskinian initiation gown if I'm not mistaken."

"Yes?" I answer, puzzled.

"I suppose it was white when they gave it to you?"

I nod.

"Look at it!"

My gown is a collage of a hundred different colors. "I must have little bits and pieces of Talents, but no deep soul gift, right?"

"Wrong. You have a deep soul gift: synesthesia. When one sense is stimulated, it causes another one to be experienced. In your case, when you hear sounds, you see colors."

"Then how come I never found my syn—synesthesia Talent before?" I ask, trying out the new word.

"I imagine it was encouraged to blossom by the sounds of singing and the music of the instruments," says Luda, arching one eyebrow. "They certainly don't have that in Noveskina."

"No—but I sang into the sound machine."

"Yes, but the sound machine collected the sounds before you had a chance to hear them." Luda shakes her head. "Anyway, your Talent is rare; it's not one the machine is programmed to recognize. The only person I've ever heard of with synesthesia is Patrice. It was because of her Talent that Patrice became the conductor for the Council. But since her death, we haven't been able to risk playing and singing all together. That's why valley folk miss her and keep her memory alive. Without her, we cannot play harmoniously, and the clashing noises can bring great harm." Luda stops chopping potatoes and gives me a wide grin. "This is so exciting, Miri! You don't know the good you can do!"

My heart leaps. I have a Talent—a really special one. I lean forward urgently. "I always thought everyone saw the sound colors."

"We usually assume that others perceive the world the way we do, but each of our viewpoints is unique. That's why we need more than One Voice. There's more than one truth, more than one right way of doing things. But," she continues, half to herself, "I can understand why none of the adults was aware of your Talent. It's such an uncommon gift. They wouldn't be expecting it, despite its value—especially to the Masker.

People often only find what they're looking for," she adds philosophically, beginning to dice another potato.

I am so excited that I ignore the potatoes that are bound to become our dinner. "This means I can be Masked as a Talented citizen instead of a house servant!"

"Masked?" Luda drops the knife into the ceramic bowl with a clang.

"Yes. Masked."

Luda doesn't even bother to pick up the knife. She just stares at me.

"Mater and Pater will be so proud of me," I babble on. "Of course, it'll be too late to be bonded with my friends, but at least they'll accept me as an equal. And I'll get to see *Darin* again! And maybe Aron—"

"You're planning to go back to Noveskina!"

"Oh, yes! Now that I have a real Talent..." the words freeze in my mouth. I suddenly remember the way the crowd fought over my labor. I narrow my eyes. "You will let me go, won't you?"

Luda wrings her hands. "The Secret Valley folk need you. They need someone with your Talent to conduct the Council."

"They don't know I have this Talent!" I snap. "Not if you don't tell them."

"I won't keep you against your will," she says slowly. "But you don't know what you're giving up. Not only for yourself, but for everyone. If we could all play together, we'd have so much strength to heal, so much ability to uplift."

I gather the potato peels and throw them into the compost. "I don't know how to conduct a Council! I can only play six notes on the flute. And I don't want to practice anymore. I want to go back to Noveskina!"

"Think what you're going back to!"

"Home."

Luda's gaze penetrates to my bones. Her bird stares at me too—his beady black eyes are more intelligent than a bird's have any right to be. "Your Talent won't grow after you are Masked."

"I can live with that."

"You're making a mistake!" cries Luda.

I shrug.

Luda slaps her forehead with her hand. "And I've been a bigger fool—assuming that you'd stay here in the Secret Valley. If I'd thought for one minute that you'd go back, I'd never have told you about Melody!"

I barely hear Luda. I am busy thinking about how I'll get home. It'll be tough to make it back without supplies or a map. "Will you help me return to Noveskina?" I beg. "Please."

Luda's hazel eyes glisten. "I can understand the temptation of living in a place of luxury with someone else to make the hard decisions, but to have your Talent limited...."

"It's not that!" I interrupt. "It's my friends and family. I miss them!"

"I sympathize with your feelings, but I'd like you to examine something before you make up your mind." She points to a strange object on a shelf. "If you still wish to go back after you've finished with it," Luda's shoulders convulse, "then I'll ask Melody to help you after she returns. But you'll have to go back the way you came. If the Masker mind-reads you to locate our valley, he won't be able to follow that route. Only someone who can actually see the ley lines can make it across—"

"How long until Melody gets back?" I interrupt, skimming my eyes over the odd hide-bound thing on the shelf.

"She'll get off soon for her annual servants' leave. Then she can take the normal route back and meet you in the deadlands."

I swallow, thinking of crossing back over the raging river. But it is summer now; the river isn't so high. *I made it once. I can do it again. Anything is worth it to get home.*

Luda continues, "Melody can get you inside the Wall. After that, you're on your own. She won't be able to go into the city again. It's been tricky for her lately, and now that you know so much, it'll be far too dangerous."

"I'd never tell on Melody," I assure Luda. "Not after the way she helped me."

"The listeners will hear you, or the Masker," answers Luda. "Are you sure you want to go back to all that?"

A small twinge of fear mars my joy, but it is far outweighed by my excitement at taking my place with my friends and family again. "Yes," I answer firmly. "I do."

Luda shakes her head with a trace of disgust in her expression, but I don't care. I am going home! As a Talented Noveskinian!

Chapter 22

THE BOOK

LUDA POINTS TO the object on the shelf. "Take your time," she says, stirring the pot of potatoes and carrots cooking over the hearth fire.

Walking past the dead Mask dangling from the wall, I try to ignore the vacant, staring eyeholes that seem to bore into the back of my head. I pick the strange, rectangular object off the shelf. As soon as I touch it, electric prickles needle my fingers. *Nerves.* The thing is heavy and smells musty.

I sit at Luda's dining table, open the strange thing, and turn the stiff, crinkled papers inside. They have writing on them just like my learning cubes. But unlike on my learning cubes, the writing doesn't move, flash, or scroll across the screen. This writing just sits on the pages, motionless. It's nearly impossible to read. I flip the strange thing closed and try to spell the static words on the front cover, letter by letter. It takes so much effort; I don't know how much time passes before I finally make out the first word: *Masks.*

Staring, I suddenly realize this is a book—a real book, like those shown in history learning cubes—and it is about Masks. I flip it back open.

The large blue letters at the top of the first page stay stubbornly still, and I can't make them out. Tilting my head to one side, I squint. For an instant the words become clear, and I can read them: *Masks: A User's Guide.*

Turning the pages eagerly, I angle the book every which way, slowly sounding out the larger words at the top of each page. *The His-tor-y of Masks, The Ma-king of Masks, The Fu-s-ing of Masks.* I stop. Mater makes Masks. It will be interesting to find out how she does it. If only it weren't so hard to decipher these impossible, motionless words.

I swing my tired head back and forth to loosen the muscles in my neck. Suddenly the letters clarify, and I am able to read them! I scan down the page about Mask making, the words flying by my eyes the way they should. But as soon as I forget to move my head, the letters stop abruptly and become indecipherable.

Swinging my head vigorously, I read: *Masks must be cloned from the cells of living human flesh. Cells harvested from the inside of the cheek immediately prior to death will yield best results in pliability and pain-responsiveness. Preserve cloned flesh in a bath of warm CH_3COOH (at 365K) until it inflates to size required.*

Yuck.

But as gross as the process sounds, it will hardly deter me from wanting to go home. I wonder how Luda expects this book to change my mind.

Reading the motionless words tires me. My head feels like it is stuffed with cotton, but I'm curious to find out more. I flip the page and read the titles to the next sections: *Candidates for Masking, The Bonding of Masks.*

I stop, recalling the Masking of my friends.

The heavy, sickening stench of sizzling flesh suddenly fills the air. I gasp for breath and drop the book. Luda glances over at me with a worried frown, but she doesn't seem to smell anything out of the ordinary. I must be tired. Taking a deep breath, I give her a shaky smile to show that I'm fine. I fight down queasiness, pick the book off the table, and open it again. Scanning through the pages, I try to find the section on bonding. My eyes finally light upon a diagram of a Mask. It connects to other Masks with colored bands like the ones I saw bonding my friends. The caption underneath directs: *It is possible to harness the voices of peoples' Talents through the Command Mask. A leader in possession of the Command Mask has only to collect Talent sound energy, linking it to become the One Voice.*

Someone has to speak for the community, I think, closing my eyes and rubbing my temples. Or there will be arguing and fighting—like I saw here in the Secret Valley. I don't agree with Luda on the importance of hearing all voices. That's what led to war in the past. And without the Masks, it will lead to war in the future. I press my palms against my burning eyeballs and then keep reading: *Wearing the Command Mask enables a leader to hear the thoughts of others. This power is amplified if the Command Mask has been recharged with the Talent energy of those being Masked and Bonded.*

Staring at those words, I feel dazed, remembering the Masker's painful grip on my arm as he heard my thoughts. In my mind, I see him in the ritual chamber, mouth open, greedily drinking in the Talent colors of my classmates, sucking in their very breath. His hair darkens, and he grows younger while my friends become listless, like the zombies in Jalene's stories. A shudder runs up my spine.

The kerosene lantern flares, flickers, and then goes out. "Pickle the Masker," Luda swears, lighting a candle. "I don't have any kerosene left. Can you read by the hearth firelight, Miri?"

Groggily, I shift down the table, closer to the fire. The smell of potato soup is stronger here. I try to read by the wavering light, but the immobile words are now even harder to make out. My eyes ache and blur. I shut the book, deciding to rest for a little while before finishing it.

Pillowing my head in my arms on the tabletop, I close my eyes. But the pain behind my eye sockets keeps throbbing. Unbidden, a vision of Mater swims through my mind. She is scraping the skin off my brother's face. Slowly, Darin turns his head toward me. His wide green eyes stare at me accusingly. I try to scream, but my throat is paralyzed, and I plummet into a heavy black slumber.

❈ ❈ ❈

Light shines through the cracks of the hut walls the next morning when Luda wakes me with a cup of potato soup.

Gulping the thick beverage, I follow Luda outside. The fresh air surrounds me with the scents of spring, and I shake off the fitful sleep of the night. "Where did you get that book?"

"It's more than just an antique book," says Luda, not quite answering my question. "It was created before the wars and impregnated with sound power. Reading it can be quite an experience."

"I know. I have to swing my head just to see the words."

"That's not quite what I mean," says Luda. "Keep reading and you'll see."

The day smells of fresh earth and grass, and I don't really feel like struggling with the weird antique. "Don't you want me to help you with the garden?"

It's more important for you to understand what that book has to say before you make your decision," replies Luda, bending to pull a thorny weed out of her flowerbeds.

"Some of it is a bit creepy, but why do you think reading about Masks will make me change my mind?"

"We'll talk about that *after* you've finished reading," replies Luda, sounding a little impatient. She walks down the stone steps and turns back to give me an encouraging smile before heading out to her garden.

Despite the smile, I can't help noticing the pinched, worried expression on her face. I watch her for a few seconds, putting off the moment when I'll have to get back to the book.

She doesn't start working right away. Instead, Luda stops and cocks her head to one side, and I know she is listening for Melody. Afterward, she sighs heavily and begins raking stones out of the soil.

There is nothing I can say to cheer her up. I turn to go back inside.

Chapter 23

A REVELATION

WHAT CAN THIS book possibly say that will change my mind? I pluck the dusty tome from the shelf once more and glance at Luda's wall painting. It is a colorful depiction of the Secret Valley. Figures talk, sing, play instruments, and dance. I trace my finger over the rough painted plaster, following blue ley lines from the Secret Valley to Noveskina.

Off in the distance is the Wall. Inside, stiff people stand with expressionless faces. If this is how she sees Noveskinians, it is no wonder she doesn't understand my reasons for wanting to go home.

But she's wrong, I think. Doesn't Luda remember the wonderful Demonstrations? The gorgeous silky gowns? The songbirds? And the food...my stomach growls to think of deep fried jellyfish and salted seaweed snacks.

I sigh and sit at the empty dining table. Opening the book to the place I left off, I swing my head a few times to bring the words into focus. Reading the book seems easier this morning: *Talents imprinted in individual voices can be collected and directed by the command Mask. Both soldiers and civilians will obey without voicing opinions or causing dissent.*

I flip the page, filled with annoyance. Luda knows there aren't any soldiers in Noveskina. The whole purpose of the

Masks is to prevent war. I scan down the following page: *Combine the strength of voices and instruments for powerful sound energies. Trumpets are—*

All at once, the book feels warm. It begins to vibrate in my hands. Alarmed, I drop it on the tabletop. *What...?* Gingerly, I reach out and touch the yellowed pages. A blast of sound fills my ears. Colors leap out at me, surrounding me in a blinding haze. When the swirling mist clears, I am standing on a hillside above a city. *Where am I? How did I get here?*

At first I'm too dizzy to notice much. Biting winds whip around my face, tangling my hair and tearing my eyes. Stumbling down the slope, trying to get away from the icy gusts, I squint, seeking shelter. The cold winds chase me, whipping my gown around my legs, pushing me further and further down the hill.

I look up and notice that I've almost reached the city gates. I also notice a group of people moving parallel to me. Mounted on elephants, they ride toward the city's rough terra-cotta walls. Others march behind them on foot. Curious, I draw closer. It looks like one of the ancient parades in the learning cubes.

Near the city, I spy more motion. Men and women sit on horses and mules with dogs yapping at their heels. They glance behind them nervously as the iron gates to the city are drawn shut with a clang. No one is smiling.

When the two groups are nearly thirty feet apart, the wind stills, and there is a sudden hush. Then people begin humming, but not all together. Each person makes a seemingly random sound, and the noises grate in a nauseating disharmony.

The colors are worse. They clash in putrid greens and lurid oranges, making me see spots. The colors could be so easy to untangle. I raise my hand to show where the green could circle more harmoniously with the blue...then drop it in utter futility.

As if beginning a ritual, a woman on an elephant begins trilling a high note. A colored ball of sound energy collects around her throat. People from both groups watch her carefully. The woman rider's voice grows shriller and then climbs to a shriek. I wince as the ball of energy rockets from her throat and plummets to smash into the front line of the opposite group.

"Counterattack!" bellows a wounded man, holding the note of his rage. The outburst of his scarlet anger strikes his opponent, toppling her from her animal. My jaw drops in astonishment. *They are fighting with their voices! Did the book bring me here? Could this be a battle of the sound wars?* The two groups come to life, and the noise and commotion is almost more than I can bear. Dogs howl, and I am overwhelmed by the constant sounds of pain. They are like nothing I have ever heard.

Overhead large black birds circle. Vultures.

Without stopping to think, I run into the middle of the fighting, shouting, "Stop! *STOP!*"

They don't stop. In fact, no one seems to see me. Another burst of scarlet anger flares toward me. I duck, but I'm not quick enough. It catches me on the side of the head, and I fall to the ground in shock.

Am I going to die here? In this book?

Within seconds, I realize that the ball of energy passed painlessly through me, striking and sizzling a woman behind me. I stand, shaking myself off, and find that I'm not hurt at all.

Suddenly there is a new sound. A sharp staccato. I recognize the shot of the drumbeat that Melody once played for me. It is a march. A new group of people reaches the walls of the city. A man with a long, black beard strides purposefully, leading his troops closer and closer.

My gaze turns to the people following him. They have the smooth skin of the Masked, and I suddenly realize that the other two groups fighting do not. Their faces are as crinkled as the ones I've grown used to in the Secret Valley. Even stranger, the Masked group carries the forbidden instruments.

The leader of the new group—I name him Blackbeard—calmly surveys the scene. A four-foot long, scaly green lizard rubs against the man's heels. Blackbeard lifts some sort of horn to his mouth and blows a flat, sour note. Gray smokes out of the horn, and my guts twist with fear.

Blackbeard lifts his hand in a signal. As one, his people raise their weapons. *"Attack!"*

The army of instruments begins to play.

Cymbals clang deafeningly. Drums beat rage into my blood. A violin sings so mournfully that my heart withers alongside the plants in the field. The other armies cringe with fear, roar with anger, cry with grief too deep to bear.

At Blackbeard's signal, the army plays louder.

The noise pounds at my brain. The deafening cacophony makes my head feel like it will explode. I stuff my fingers into my ears, but the hideous din continues. Animals scream, trying to run. Colors blow up around me. The earth burns and blackens beneath my feet. Worst of all is the jagged stream of sound that flows from Blackbeard's throat; it wraps around the voices of his soldiers, braiding their colors together with those of the blasting instruments, collecting them all into one black beam.

It isn't bright. It isn't beautiful. It is the dense, angry combination of all colors. It seems to draw me in. And even though it makes my head throb to look at it, I watch, with horrified fascination, as the beam shrinks into Blackbeard's throat and disappears.

The battlefield is suddenly as dark and silent as a crypt. I blink with disbelief. The fighting between groups rages on, and the army of instruments still plays, but it is as if all noise has been sucked out of the air. And all color with it.

Then Blackbeard opens his mouth and a black beam rolls from his throat, roaring like thunder, hitting the battlefield in a sonic boom that makes the earth shake. Trees burst into fire. Sections of the wall crumble. Bodies fall around me, disintegrating before my eyes. Flames rise from the tattered remnants of their clothing. A revolting charred smell fills the air.

Horror chokes me.

A rainbow of beautiful colors—the full spectrum of sound—rises from the ashes and floats gently over to Blackbeard. It hovers around him, coalescing into a stream of light. He opens his mouth and drinks in the voices of the dead.

Bile rises in my throat, filling me with the rotten taste of decay.

Blackbeard grows larger, taller, brimming with vibrancy. His face glows with pleasure, his black eyes sparkling with joy. Surviving soldiers from the first two groups fight to turn their animals, trying to flee. Others run, heedless of being trampled.

Blackbeard smiles. *"Attack!"* Instantly, his army raises its instruments, and the whole terrifying scene begins again.

I can't watch this a second time. I feel sick. Suddenly, everything starts to spin. Colors blend together, blurring everything into a white haze. I can't move. All I can do close my eyes and hope that it is all some strange nightmare. Hope that this horror of war never existed and will never be real.

The mists part, and I find myself sitting at Luda's dining table, the book open in front of me. I slam it shut and shove it violently across the rough wood surface. My stomach heaves, and I push myself away from the table, leaning over and retching again and again, trying to purge myself of the gruesome spectacle.

"It can't be true," I whisper. But I know it is. The image from the secret Masking ritual is fixed in my head. I *saw* the Masker drink in the voices of my friends, just as Blackbeard did to his soldiers. And using the power of their voices, just like Blackbeard, he could use them to go to war.

My stomach knots with further understanding: *How else could the Masker convince Mater to make a servant's mask for her own daughter? How else could he convince everyone to turn a blind eye to my disappearance?* The Masker already controls everyone. He already manipulates them like puppets. My friends. My family.

And Darin is next in line to be Masked. *"No!"* I croak.

Chapter 24

MAKING PICTURES

LUDA COMES IN and kneels beside me. "You've experienced the sound wars."

"It's not true!" I sob. "It can't be."

"It's true."

I gaze at the offending book. "How did you get it?"

Luda shrugs. "Filched it from the Masker right before I ran away."

"But why?"

Luda stands, finding a clean cloth to help me wipe my face. "I wanted to know how he stole our voices."

Something scratches at the cottage door.

"What's that?" I ask anxiously.

Luda's face lights up. She skips to the door and flings it open.

A dog bounds in, wagging his tail.

"Woof! Is it really you?" I run over and give the dog a big hug.

Luda peers out, squinting against slants of morning sunshine. "Where is Melody?" asks Luda. "Isn't she with you, Harry?"

I smile, looking at Woof. His real name is Harry! I should have guessed—the dog is so shaggy. He thumps his tail, slobbering my face in joyful greeting. I scratch between his ears the way he likes.

Luda cocks her head and concentrates in her familiar way. "It's no use. I still can't hear her. And now Harry is back— without Melody. She's overdue for her leave, and Harry never returns without her." Luda paces the small room; then she strides over to an old basket. She pulls out a silver Noveskinian gown—the kind only Important Officials wear.

I watch her slip the gown over her head and put the last of the winter apples into her woven pack and lay her wooden oboe, carefully wrapped in a shawl, on top.

"Where are you going?"

"To Noveskina," answers Luda. "Something is wrong. I can feel it. Melody needs me." Luda adds some cheese and bread to her pack. "You can stay here," she says, heading out the door.

"Wait!" I cry, my thoughts speeding. The idea of returning to Noveskina is suddenly terrifying. But I owe it to Melody to try to help her. And, in the back of my mind, I hold a secret hope that I have enough time to warn Darin about the Masks. To tell him the truth before it is too late. "I'm coming with you."

"No," replies Luda. She lifts her chin. "I can't believe you still want to return to Noveskina after what you've seen, but you'll just have to wait. I'm going to have enough on my hands trying to rescue Melody."

"You don't understand! I don't want to go back and be Masked—not ever! I *know* the book is true. I saw the Masker recharge. I *saw* it at the Masking of my friends!" I pause, everything becoming clear, "And the Masker knew it. That's why I had to escape. And Melody helped me."

Luda pours a heap of seed into the cockatiel's bowl. "Then all the more reason for you to stay here where you'll be safe."

"But you can't hear Melody now. How will you find her? If

you take me, maybe I can help." My words tumble out in a rush, filled with my sudden urgency to go.

Luda strokes her bird's delicate neck with her thumb. "You'll have to stay here," she tells the cockatiel. "We can't risk you squawking at the wrong time."

The bird hops over to his bowl. His black eyes glitter with understanding.

It takes me a second longer to register her words. She said "we"! Throwing my cloak over my shoulder, I follow her out the door. Before we head off, she stops in front of the chicken coop and sets the animals free to roost in a tree. "Forage for yourselves," she tells the clucking birds.

Then Luda turns and takes off so fast that I have to jog to keep up. I know she is too anxious about Melody to let me slow her down, so I chase after her. Brambles grab at my gown and my ankle turns in a pothole. "Luda," I pant. "What kind of raised voices make a Mask come off? How did you get your Mask off? I know you hate to talk about it, but you have to tell me. My friends are Masked—and my brother will be Masked soon—and if there is any way I can help them get the Masks off...."

It is a while before she speaks. "Raised voices aren't the only way to strip a Mask. Hearing certain sounds can do it.... But you'll only be able to help your friends if they want to be helped," she says, interrupting her own train of thought. "Still I might as well tell you the whole story. Telling it can't upset me any more than I already am." She sighs, slowing down to a brisk walk.

"You can't imagine what it's like being a listener—hearing other people's thoughts and feelings. When I became pregnant...." Luda winces, as if the memory is painful.

"What happened?"

"Female listeners shouldn't have babies. Pregnancy enhances our Talent to the point where we can't shut it off. Even with the dampening powers of a Mask, we're constantly bombarded by everyone's thoughts and feelings." As she speaks, I imagine Luda, large with pregnancy, suffering as people's emotions stab into her like so many sharp knives.

"I was in such a raw state, so vulnerable to everyone's emotions. When I found the book—it was too much to learn at one time." She walks quietly for a minute before continuing. I stay silent, following her to the knoll overlooking the valley where we first talked and watched the sunset. Luda walks down the hill, but turns to the left to take a small, rocky path instead of continuing toward the town square.

When she speaks again, her voice trembles with passion. "Masks—as *military weapons!* I think it was the shock of that, the outrage I felt in realizing the Masker was *lying*. He wasn't being the One Voice to maintain harmony. He was using us, using our voices—stealing them—living off our energy." Luda spits. "All he ever wanted was to keep us weak so that he could be in control."

Luda shakes her head. "When I realized this, I screamed and screamed. The power of my shock is what peeled my Mask off."

Shock. Suddenly I remember the way Jalene's voice cracked through her Mask when she thought I betrayed her sanctuary. Her anger made her Mask sizzle at the corners. "Did it hurt?"

"Yes, it did."

I want to ask more, but Luda looks so sad that I hold my questions.

After that, we trudge in heavy silence. Every once in a

while, Luda cocks her head to one side and listens for Melody, but I know she doesn't hear anything. Her worry is so palpable that it thickens the air.

At last we hit a smooth, dirt road and the going is easier. We pass a cottage. The rich brown tones of a guitar spill outside. Then the vermilion from a man's tenor joins in.

Luda stops. "They shouldn't be playing and singing together like that! Not without a conductor." She strides toward the man and woman seated on a small cottage porch. "Come along, I have to talk to them."

After reading the book, I know all too well what danger noise can bring. But the vermilion tones that hover next to the earthy colors of the guitar are pretty. I lift my hands, conscious of how the colors should weave together. As we walk toward the couple, my fingers flow in a dance of their own as I grasp strands of each color, sculpting and twining the yellowish red with the deep auburn. A holographic picture of the cozy house shimmers in the air. I stand back, pleased at my creation.

The man stops singing. "What's that?"

"She did it!" the woman exclaims. "She took our sounds and turned them into pictures."

"The way Patrice could," her companion adds thoughtfully. "Could she learn to conduct the Council?"

I turn to Luda, confused. I thought I was the only one who could see sounds. *Why can they see my picture? And how can it be enough to conduct the Council?*

"Yes, she could," Luda answers the woman, putting her arm around my shoulder. "But first, Miri and I have to go to Noveskina."

The woman sets down her guitar. "You can't take her away. She's too valuable."

"I have to," Luda says grimly. "Melody is in trouble."

The man steps forward and grabs my arm. "This child is far too important to risk!" The vermilion around his throat turns to a muddy maroon.

Luda wrings her hands in anguish. "I may need Miri. I don't know if I can do it without her help."

"You're being selfish, Luda!" hisses the woman. "The loss of this child would be worse for the valley folk than the loss of Melody."

Luda gasps as if someone has slugged her in the stomach. Pain seeps from her in clouds of gray. *The insensitive woman! Can't she see how she is hurting Luda?*

I realize she cannot.

I raise my arms, shaping Luda's pain until it becomes a portrait of Melody. I give her a servant's Mask, shaping the sharp prongs, digging them into Melody's smooth skin. Piercing it.

Luda gives a cry of grief, but I continue. I want this man and woman to understand.

Taking the other woman's earthy colors, I form a cloak, weaving in the cloudiness of Luda's pain and fear. I drape the colors over the woman's shoulders so that she may feel their burden.

The woman gasps and clutches her chest. "Take her then," she says softly.

"You're making a mistake!" exclaims the man.

The woman shakes her head and he releases my arm.

"Please, please bring her back," says the woman.

"I will," promises Luda.

Chapter 25

JOURNEY BACK

"LUDA, WHAT DID I do? How did I make those pictures?"

"Your Talent," says Luda. "It must be evolving."

"What does that mean?" I ask. "I thought my Talent was to see the colors, not make images. And why could they see them?"

"You aren't Masked, so your Talent will grow. And it is becoming more and more like Patrice's. She knew how to arrange everyone's colors to make something beautiful. This is the conductor's job. You can help people, show them what they are capable of doing, creating, feeling."

I chew on the idea for a while, and it takes me a minute to notice that we have come to the end of the valley. A tall metal gate, pocked with age, crosses from cliff face to cliff face, completely blocking our path. Luda takes out an old fashioned key and turns it in the hole. The gate creaks open, and I see the river. The water is still high with early summer run-off. But here, the river meanders lazily instead of crashing between rocks. There is a small boat tied up in the shallows.

Luda shuts and locks the gate, then tucks the key back into her robe. She strides to the riverbank and quickly unties the boat. Harry leaps into the vessel. Luda turns to me. "Come on."

Stepping carefully into the center, I feel the boat rock back and forth beneath my feet. Luda steps in, hands me an oar, and we row across in silence. It is so easy and effortless compared to my previous crossing. Working together, we reach the other bank in no time. We tie the boat up in the shadows of a small forest. Then we begin to walk.

We walk and we walk. We don't stop to eat. We just gobble dried fruit and nuts as we hike. Luda does not even let us stop to sleep. My rubber legs tremble and wobble as we march over the scorched earth of the deadlands. I keep looking up to check for flyers, but there aren't any. No one is looking for me anymore.

By the early morning of the next day, we fight through the last blackberry thistles and arrive at the Wall just as the night sky has begun to lighten. "Record time," Luda says with satisfaction. "We made it in less than two days."

Exhausted, I don't say anything.

Luda circles around the Wall until we come to the unmonitored gate. She turns to Harry. "Stay!" she orders before fitting her palm against the slight indentation.

"Important Official here."

My eyes widen. Sticking close to her back, I scurry through the recognition door. Harry shoots through an instant before the Wall closes. He sits at our feet, wagging his tail.

Luda shakes her head. "I don't know what got into that dog. Harry always obeys." She tries listening for a minute, then shakes her head and turns to me. "Where do you think Melody is?"

Harry pricks his ears and takes a few steps as if to say, "Follow me."

So we do. We weave our way through the overgrown alleys and winding backstreets of Noveskina, deep into the heart of the city. At last, we reach a mesh enclosure that I've seen before. "The aviary," whispers Luda.

"How are we going to get through the mesh?"

Harry answers my question by starting to dig. Squatting beside the dog, I begin the tedious task of scooping up soil.

It takes the three of us over an hour to excavate a hole barely big enough to squeeze through one at a time. By the time we all wriggle our way in, the sun has peeked its way over the horizon. But we are in.

Our sudden entrance startles the birds. Alarmed, they whistle and flit, lighting up the morning sky with a kaleidoscope of spinning song colors. We freeze, praying that no one in the house will hear the commotion.

Eventually, the birds calm down, and we creep through the jungly growth. Harry leads us closer to the door. Fortunately, the ferns provide good cover as we make our way closer to the lattice door. It's strange: the globe lights inside the house are on and the door is wide open.

"Stay, Harry," whispers Luda.

The dog pricks his ears, thumps his tail, and whines softly, but this time he obeys.

Luda and I tiptoe inside. It is so awful being back in this elegant house. My skin is clammy and my knees quake, but I force myself to go on.

We stop in the hallway for a moment, listening for the Masker or Melody. Although the house is lit up, we do not hear anyone moving about. Cautiously, we look everywhere on the main floor, even the cooking room and the closets. There is no sign of life. We creep upstairs and quietly search every room. They are all empty.

Luda clenches her hands so tightly that her knuckles turn white. "It's no use. She isn't here."

Chapter 26

A SEARCH FOR MELODY

DEFEATED, WE HEAD back to the main hallway. We can't risk spending any more time in the Masker's house now that the sun has come up. As we turn to the aviary door, I notice a subtle rose light seeping out from the edges of another doorway. I've seen this color before. "Here!" I point excitedly. "She's behind this door somewhere. She's in the tunnels!"

But then I recall my early attempts at escaping this house. The door to the tunnels was always locked.

Luda steps past me and places her hand on the recognition lock. "Luda here," it intones. I gasp. Why does one of the Masker's locks recognize Luda? Who *is* she?

But there's no time to ask. Luda pulls me through, and once again I find myself in the dark tunnels. Unsure of which scent to follow, I wait for my eyes to adjust. A dim glow of rose flowers in the blackness.

I'd recognize that shade of rose anywhere. The floating light brightens as we follow it farther down the tunnel. And then, suddenly, I can hear humming. Melody! Her voice is raw, desperate.

"Increase the electric pulse rate!" orders a muffled male voice. The words come from behind a thick tapestry. I recognize the wall hanging as the one that covered the ritual room doorway.

"We are already at peak intensity," answers a young female. "The gauge shows us at highest pulse rate, but for some reason it's not working. The prongs of her Mask must be faulty. They aren't triggering the appropriate nerve-pain response. She should be in agony."

Luda gives me a tormented look. "Now you'll see how listeners are used in Noveskina."

I shudder, thinking of the pain Melody is about to endure. "Should we go in?"

"Wait," Luda whispers back. "I have to listen to their thoughts—figure out who is in there. If there's someone who knows me, I might have a plan." She cocks her head to one side and concentrates.

Melody's humming falters with fatigue.

"I hear her now," exclaims a male. "She...she's not wearing a Mask!"

"That's why there's been no response to the electric pulses," answers the woman.

"Never mind," says another woman's voice. "The Masker will find another way to punish her. We must still discover why she disobeyed."

Melody tries to hum again, but her voice cracks.

"One, two, three, four..." says the male. "She's counting to cover her thoughts."

"If you concentrate and focus hard enough, you can find the subliminal thoughts below the counting," directs the female voice.

"She's been smuggling...instruments."

"To a valley?"

There is a hoarse croak as Melody fights to resume her

humming, fights to keep the listeners out.

"They've been making copies," adds a new voice. This male sounds hesitant. It's a voice I know.

Melody begins to hum again, her voice rattling. I know she can't keep it up. *In a few minutes, they will hear everything. They'll know how to find the Secret Valley.*

"Who was that?" asks a female. "There's someone else here!"

I throw Luda an urgent look. She nods, moving the woven tapestry aside.

We barge into the ritual chamber.

Melody is trapped in the center of a circle of listeners. They are all raised up on soft cushions. She is hunched below them on the bare floor. Red wires connect to her body with sticky white pads. They cover her forehead, temples, throat, and wrists. The wires lead to a large, black machine that puts out a constant, dull growl.

Melody's whole body is listless, caved in. She droops with exhaustion, and there is a hunted, tortured look in her eyes. But she continues to hum valiantly.

The listeners turn on their pillows and stare at us, disbelief on their faces. I recognize one member of the circle. He flinches, his wide violet eyes giving me a brief pleading look of shame as I shoot him a look of disgust.

"I didn't have a choice," says Ceiron. Sweat drips off his brow, and he looks like he's going to be sick. "If I'd known...."

Luda confidently addresses the oldest of the group. "Hello, Ori."

"Luda?" asks the elderly man. "It has been years. Where have you been?"

"I'm afraid that is confidential, Ori. You can apply to be

briefed by the Masker." Luda's tone is so convincing that I almost believe her. "He has ordered me to retrieve the prisoner."

"You can't do that!" protests a young female. "We haven't finished listening."

"It's all right," says the old man. "We know her."

An older woman agrees, "Yes. She has authority."

Luda slips between two listeners and goes straight to Melody. "I'm here, now, baby," she whispers. "It's all over. Come with me." She gently lifts Melody from the floor.

The listeners stare at Luda, dumbfounded, as she leads Melody out of the circle, but nobody makes a move to stop her.

The three of us head into the tunnel. Once I slip the tapestry back into place, we break into an awkward run, draping Melody's arms over our shoulders for support.

We are halfway down the dark passageway when I hear a commotion erupt in the ritual chamber. Colored strands of dissent filter into the tunnel.

"I *heard* her!"

"Luda has seniority."

"But she called the prisoner *baby!*"

"Follow them!"

"Hurry!" whispers Luda. Muscles in my side cramp and squeeze as we run. Multiple smells roil around me.

Our pursuers' pounding feet echo loudly against the walls. But they take the wrong tunnel. I breathe again. We have a chance.

"The other way!" cries a faintly ringing voice. Footsteps turn back in our direction. "They're heading towards the crypt!"

I squeeze Luda's arm, alarmed.

"No thoughts," Luda whispers. "Just follow." Abruptly, she

changes direction, going down a narrow side tunnel that smells like old shoes.

Breathing a relieved sigh, I listen to the footsteps receding in the opposite direction. We sheer around a corner and out into a larger tunnel. Staggering under Melody's weight, I gulp air. It is a while before I recognize the lemon trail.

"But the park is crowded," I whisper.

"Melody can't climb the hill to the unused gate. And there will be no one at the park at this hour."

Melody pants.

"Are you in a lot of pain, baby?" asks Luda.

"Only a...little...headache...."

"The other way! They took the other tunnel!" cries a distant voice. Pounding footsteps grow louder.

"Faster!" urges Luda.

Pulling Melody the last steps through the dim passageway, I can still hear the listeners only a tunnel behind us as we dash out from the underground and crawl behind some flowering shrubs. Melody collapses onto the ground. "We'll have to let her rest for a few seconds." Luda glances apprehensively at the tunnel. "I can't carry her, and she's so weak."

While we wait for Melody to catch her breath, I peer through the branches. Bright songbirds flutter from bough to bough, tweeting merrily. A crowd is gathered around the stage. My heart sinks. "It was a mistake to come here. They're having a morning performance."

"Perfect," whispers Luda. "The listeners won't be able to hear us in this crowd, and everyone will be so busy watching the show that no one will notice us. As soon as Melody can get up, we'll make a run for the Wall—there will be many farmers coming through the door to see the new Talent. We should be able to slip right by them. Then we can hide among the farmers' stalls on the other side of the Wall.

My eyes flick back and forth between the audience and the tunnel where, any minute, I expect the listeners to bust forth.

As I stare at the stage, my heart breaks to see so many familiar faces. Eris hovers over the crowd. Mater and Pater sit up front with the Masker. I even see Jalene quietly chatting with Nonce only fifteen feet away. Her gown has faded from the rich, deep purple to a washed-out lavender.

Luda rubs Melody's temples. "Can you stand yet?"

My heart beats faster. Darin sits at the back with his age-mates. Darin! Perhaps there is time to warn him. To tell him everything. Reaching my arms out to him, I take a step out from behind the large bush.

Luda yanks me back. "What are you doing?" she hisses. "Do you want to get us caught?"

Shaking my head, I chide myself for being so stupid. Luda is right. Darin will have to wait.

Luda points. "Let's crawl behind these trees until we're closer to the Wall—then we'll run."

I creep after Luda and Melody, grateful that people are too engrossed in the upcoming performance to pay any attention to us. But a crackle of twigs announces the entrance of our pursuers into the park. Luda, Melody, and I melt into the dappled shadows beneath the trees.

Ceiron's voice rings out loud and clear, "They couldn't have come this way. All these people would have seen them."

My heart beats wildly with hope.

"Nonsense," says another listener. "People are preparing for the performance. They didn't even turn when we came through."

"He's right," agrees another. "Better search the park."

Footsteps fan out. Some come our way.

"Run!" orders Luda.

We sprint in the direction of the Wall, dragging Melody along.

"There they are!" shouts a listener.

I feel a hundred eyes burning into my back as the crowd turns to watch us flee. "Hurry, Melody," I beg. "Please hurry."

"I'm trying," she pants.

Footsteps pound after us. Glancing over my shoulder, I see Darin at the front of the pack. I almost lose my footing.

"Come on," urges Luda.

She reaches the Wall first and hurriedly places her hand against the recognition lock. The door does not open.

Luda takes her hand away and fits it back again more carefully. "Open!"

No response.

Chapter 27

BURIED ALIVE

"WHY DOESN'T IT recognize me?" wails Luda. Tears fill her eyes.

Darin arrives in the lead. He isn't even out of breath.

"Darin!" I plead. "Help!"

My brother only lowers his eyebrows. "You ran away," he says. His voice sounds deeper than I remember. "Where have you been?"

"It was the only thing I could do. I wanted to tell you."

His eyes flicker with doubt.

"Darin, they were going to Mask me as a—"

Flanked by his circle of listeners, the Masker strides over to us, cutting me off. He clears his throat. "How nice to see you again, Luda," he says with exaggerated courtesy. "If you'd stayed in Noveskina, where you belong, you'd have known that we now change the recognition keys on the door in the park Wall regularly."

Luda thrusts her chest out and her chin up. She looks almost large. "Let us out—now."

The crowd stands in a half circle behind the Masker, murmuring restlessly.

Pater hurries over to the Masker. "What seems to be the problem?" Then he sees me. His cheeks flush and his eyes glitter. "Miri!"

The Masker gives him a warning look. "Control your voice, Uri."

Pater asks in a bland tone, "Where have you been?"

The Masker leans forward. Clearly, he, too, is interested in where I've been.

"In the deadlands—only they aren't all dead," I lie.

Pater gives me a searching look.

"And we want to go back. Pater, help me!"

The Masker glowers. "This is my decision. Uta!" he calls. "Come here. Miri is back."

"Back from running away and disgracing us," says Mater, limping through the crowd. She throws me a look of disgust.

Luda faces the Masker and speaks in a rock-hard voice. "Let us out. You have no right to keep us."

"As I recall, I have every right," says the Masker, his black eyes deadly calm. "You, Luda, are my life partner. You should have stayed with me. And worse, you ran away—pregnant—with my child!"

The Masker turns to Melody. "This must be her." He takes Melody's limp arm.

My knees go weak at the revelation.

"Why didn't you tell me, my dear?" the Masker asks Melody. "Didn't you know I was your pater?"

"I knew," replies Melody, her voice bitter.

The Masker continues unperturbed. "You must be brilliantly Talented to have kept me from *hearing* you for so long." He gives a wry half-smile. "As I would expect from my offspring," he continues. "You were to be my successor as the One Voice."

Melody cringes.

The Masker strokes his bushy black beard. "My recharges aren't lasting as long as they used to." His smile crystallizes my blood. I know too well what he does to recharge. "I've served Noveskina for generations now. But I can't go on forever. It will be time for a replacement soon."

"Not me," rasps Melody.

"No, certainly not," agrees the Masker cordially. "Luda has ruined you, and you haven't had the training. Most unfortunate," he sighs. "Fate has not worked out to your advantage. Besides," he says, turning to me. "I've already used the power of my voice to give Darin my command Talent."

I glance at Darin, confused.

Darin smiles. "I knew there was something extraordinary about my Talent." The pleased lilt in his voice makes me shiver.

"How did you charge Darin?" asks Pater. I've never heard his voice so carefully controlled.

The Masker smoothes his tinselly gold gown. "Actually, we charged both your children, but the experiment failed with Miri."

My mouth is dry. I stare at Mater. "You experimented on me? Like I was some sort of *rat?*"

Mater nods, unruffled. "When I was pregnant, the Masker sang into a sound printer placed against my belly. We were trying to pass you his command Talent, but something went wrong."

"What went wrong?" asks Pater quietly. A fine-hair split runs down the edge of Pater's Mask.

"It wasn't enough. It didn't work," says Mater curtly. "And when the Masker charged Darin, we over-calculated. The excess sound energy erupted from the machine and ripped down my legs and his—"

"That's why you're both crippled!" I blurt, making the

connection for the first time.

"Yes. And why you turned out to be just as disappointing as your pater," Mater spits.

The crowd murmurs at this insult.

The hairline crack running down Pater's Mask widens. "*I'm disappointing?*" His face twists into a hideous grimace. "*You never asked my permission to experiment on my children!*"

"Lower your voice, Uri," Mater says complacently. She pats her flyaway red hair into place. "You didn't need to know."

"These are *my* children," accuses Pater, his voice rising. "You are my life partner. You should have asked. You should have at least told the truth about your leg."

Pater's Mask blisters. The weakened cracks grow into fissures, and I can see the raw, red skin of his face underneath. Several people back away.

"Lower your voice, Uri," snaps the Masker.

"I have every right to speak up about *my own children!*" shouts Pater. The right cheek of his Mask sizzles off in one large flake.

"The Masker lied to Uri," sobs Ceiron. "A lie of omission." His face contorts with the pain he is hearing. "The Masker lied once, maybe more."

The people shift their feet restlessly like a herd of animals preparing to stampede.

The Masker holds his head high. "With the One Voice and for your own good. I know. I was there during the sound wars. There is no peace without absolute control."

It hits me like a blinding white wave. I hadn't made the connection because the sound wars happened so long ago. But it is the same black beard, the same man. "It was you!" I accuse. "You were the one in the book. The one who stole everyone's voice and created that hideous beam. The destruction of the sound wars—all of the death—it was you!"

The people cover their ears and moan.

"You're upsetting people with your silly ideas," warns the Masker. He turns to the crowd. "Don't listen to their lies. Lock the three of them in the crypt!"

A chill runs down my spine.

"No!" shrieks Pater, reaching for me. "They'll be buried alive in those tombs. Your own daughter."

"I've spent my whole life working to keep the unity," says the Masker in his sickeningly calm voice. "One song, one story, One Voice. Sacrifices must be made." The Masker places his palms on his temples as if he is trying to think, and then he sings one sustained note. The bands of bonding that connect everyone's voice to the Masker's become clearly visible.

"Lock them in the crypt!" repeats the Masker.

A dozen Noveskinians stride over to us, ready to do his bidding. My friends, my age-mates, Nonce, Aron, Jalene, Eris, are at the front of the group. Only Ceiron hangs back.

"Jalene," I cry, "no!"

Her face remains impassive, unemotional.

Pressing my back into the Wall, I watch as my friends mercilessly advance.

Suddenly the rich amber tones of an oboe soar through the air. Luda! As if in answer, the songbirds flitting through the leafy trees chirrup and cheep.

A gasp ripples through the crowd.

"Stop!" booms the Masker. "That instrument is dangerous!" But Luda isn't Masked, and she doesn't listen to him.

"Liar!" I yell. "It's not the instruments that are dangerous, only how they are used." Turning away from my friends, I lift my hands and concentrate. Luda's playing has bought me some time. I direct the color from Luda's tune into a three-dimensional picture that I pray everyone will see.

"It's the Masker," exclaims Eris, "but he's old."

"No one may see me old and remember!" roars the Masker.

Ceiron's face puckers in a frown. "I remember," he whispers softly.

The Masker makes a long, low sound. It rolls out of his throat in a thin black beam. He aims it—straight at me.

Ducking fast, I roll to the ground an instant before it hits. The beam crisps the hair on the back of my head and then smacks the Wall.

Crack. A shot like thunder. A huge stone blows from the Wall and thuds to the ground, releasing an avalanche of smaller stones. The crowd scatters in terror. Some people double over in pain, begging the Masker to stop. I crawl behind the rubble, hiding from the Masker's searching gaze.

"Careful," Mater warns the Masker. "You know the Wall is defenseless against sounds from the inside."

"Farmers here," intones the recognition lock. A new group of people races into the park. "What's going on?" asks the man in the lead. "The Wall is crumbling."

"Halt!" commands the Masker.

Obediently, they stop right between me and the Masker. I exhale. Peeping out from behind the fallen rock, I see the farmers mixed in with people carrying awkwardly shaped bundles. People with sun-crinkled skin. The Secret Valley folk!

"Where is Luda?" demands the whiskery old woman. "We've come to get Luda and Melody and Miri."

"Farmers, out!" commands the Masker, pointing to the gap in the Wall.

The farmers begin to move, but the old woman pulls out a ceramic drum and begins tapping a steady beat. "We'll leave when you give us our people."

The Masker holds his hands over his ears and bellows, "Out of the question. Seize them!"

Aron and Nonce, standing closest to the Masker, move to obey, hypnotically weaving through the crowd.

I tap the old woman's shin. She stops playing. "Mir—" I put my finger to my lips to silence her, but it is too late.

The Masker spies me.

"Keep playing," I beg. The old woman throws me a curious look, but she continues to beat, beat, beat. I gather the shimmering orange color and stretch it out with my hands until it becomes a shining, round disc.

The Masker sings a sharp, dark note and directs his beam at me.

Instinctively, I hold up my orange shield. The beam hits, knocking me to the ground. But my defense works, and the sound energy boomerangs, flying back to the Masker. He reels from the impact and the hair around his temples whitens.

But he stands quickly, a frightening smile on his face. "It will take more than that, Miri." He begins to sing. His voice is dark and seductive. "One Voice, one song, one life, one verse...." Only I can see the notes of his song gathering the murky colors of the crowd's confusion. The noises condense into one enormous black ball of energy that slowly shrinks into the Masker's throat.

My mouth goes dry as everything around begins to grow silent. The world fades to black and white.

Chapter 28

THE SYMPHONY

THERE IS ONE last, desperate thing I can try. Gathering my courage, I yell, "Play the instruments—now—all together!" My voice echoes through the vacuum created by the Masker.

"Too risky," protests Rafe. "That much uncontrolled sound could destroy us all."

The blackness around the Masker's throat deepens. Slowly, he collects all the stolen voices of Noveskina.

"I'll conduct. Like Patrice."

Secret Valley folks clasp their instruments, but nobody plays. They look at me doubtfully.

"Hurry!" I shout. "It's our only chance."

Hesitantly at first, the man with the vermilion voice begins to sing. I beckon to him, drawing out his voice, making it stronger.

Rafe joins him, tapping his drums. But he is out of rhythm.

Luda plays a note on her oboe. The sound clashes with Rafe's drumming. A woman strums her guitar; the key jangles discordantly. A cymbal clangs harshly. As more and more Secret Valley folks pull out their instruments, the noise grows. This isn't what we need. *They can't see the colors. They can't see how they collide and jar.*

The Masker's gloating laugh fills the air. The darkness around him expands, shriveling the leaves of the birch tree over his head.

The cacophony grows as the people of the Secret Valley increase the frenzy of their playing in a desperate attempt to stop him. *They don't know this only makes him stronger. Only I can see the sound colors being sucked into his throat.*

Raising my hands, I try to direct the music, try to conduct. But the colors of the instruments spin wildly toward the Masker, getting tangled up in his beam. His voice is just too strong.

Then he opens his mouth and aims farther down the Wall—straight at Luda.

"No!" I shout.

As the black beam burns past me, I jump and grab it. The skin of my hands blisters and peels, but I hold on stubbornly. Using one hand to slow the beam, I tear at it with the other. It pulls apart in strands of color like pieces of tangled yarn.

"Stop her!" snarls the Masker.

For once nobody does as he orders.

My hands seem to know what to do as I unravel the beam, pulling each color out and putting it aside.

The Masker's face reddens with rage. "I said *stop her!*" he yells.

I ignore him. I ignore my raw, bloodied hands and keep working. When the beam is a mere thread of black, I take the colors I've liberated and begin to weave, placing fuchsia next to violet, entwining teal with silver, limning cobalt with yellow, knitting strands of sound together into a harmony of color, light, and air.

Even though they can't see the colors, the Secret Valley folk watch me carefully. They follow my hand signals with their instruments and respond to my cues with the exact colors I require.

"Grab the instruments!" the Masker shouts. "They will destroy the unity. Destroy Noveskina!"

Aron reaches for Selma's harp, but hesitates. I take the Masker's black note, soften it with white from a chime, and tuck the gray mist gently back into the lavender. The Masker's voice wavers, and Aron drops his hand.

Songbirds tweet along with us, and I plait the strands of their song into my illustration. Harry runs into the crowd, yelping madly. I weave his voice into the tapestry. The sounds of instruments and singing grow, building, twining around each other. Notes speak back and forth, duets play games of question and answer, and complex arrangements are like discussions shared; we play in a joyous symphony.

Around us, Masks pop, peeling off flesh. Ceiron's comes off in large chunks, leaving the skin beneath looking exposed and pink. I use the orange shriek of his pain to accent the note beside the soothing harp refrain.

The bands connecting Ceiron to Eris snap.

The Masker's beard grays. "This is chaos, disaster, war!" he rasps. As each band breaks, the Masker loses some of his power. His voice weakens as he grows older. My hands work deftly, embellishing the Masker's discord with the trilling sounds of the birds, so that they enhance and contrast his minor key.

The airy hologram I design grows into a mesmerizing whirl of color. People stare as I recreate my memory of the Council. I sculpt a group of people; sound colors flow from each individual, sparkling and dancing, united in discussion.

The band between Eris and Jalene ruptures. Their voices leave the Masker, and he ages a little further, his face pocked, his body crumbling.

Lifting my arms, I bring the sound to a blissful crescendo.

As their Masks fall, people howl with pain and then cry with joy. For the first time in history, Noveskinians lift their voices in chorus, forcing the last bands of bondage to sever. Their voices are rusty from disuse, but their notes are pure.

"Darin!" croaks the Masker, decaying before our eyes. He gives one last gasp before centuries of stolen voices finally drain away from him. His body dissolves into dust, leaving only his squirming Mask wriggling on the ground.

Mater grabs the command Mask and throws it toward my brother. "Quick, Darin! Put it on while it's still alive."

Darin catches the Mask and looks at it. Temptation fights with disgust on his face.

"We need *one* strong voice to lead us," urges Mater. "It's your Talent—the rest of our voices must be given in service to you. It will prevent destruction—war!"

"Would you rather speak alone than have all this?" I ask Darin, sweeping my arms over the dancing, singing, crying, laughing crowd.

Darin looks at the rainbow of color floating through the crowd, then at the slimy slick of flesh in his hands. He drops the Mask to the ground. "No."

"You're making a mistake, Darin!" hisses Mater, swooping down to pluck the Mask from the ground. "Think of the position, of the power you're giving up. Think of the *good* you could do."

"What was the good of trying to kill my sister?" asks Darin.

Mater opens her mouth to argue, but her words are drowned by Darin lifting his voice to the sky and singing the purest golden note I've ever heard. I look up and watch it shimmering above us like a promise of peace.

"How are we going to live without the Masks?" Jalene asks shyly, coming up beside me. Her skin is burned and raw, but her faded lilac gown has brightened to its original shade of vivid purple.

Leaning back against the cool Wall, I try to think of an answer. I remember how my time in Noveskina failed to reveal my soul gift. My Talent wasn't recognized. There was no room for it. No room for me or my individuality.

"We'll each have to find out for ourselves," I tell her. "We'll still develop our own Talents. But we'll have to find our own voices and learn to share them equally. I know what we'll discover if we do. We'll have something stronger than the One Voice.

Lifting my hands, I wait.

Slowly the babbling of the crowd grows quiet and people turn to watch me. I gesture for the Secret Valley folks to pick up their instruments. Then I lower my hands to conduct. Instruments and voices lift to the sky in a harmony more complete than any One Voice could ever be.

"We will have music."

More **Lobster Press** Teen Reads

...from the Millennium Generation Series

Make Things Happen:
The Key to Networking for Teens
by Lara Zielin
▸ ISBN 1-894222-43-1

Discover the endless opportunities that are just a conversation away! This book is a reliable guide with important details like why we network, where to network, and how to overcome those networking nerves.

"Any teenager who has ever been asked what they want to do after high school will be far better equipped to answer after reading and applying the networking wisdom of Lara Zielin." – *Independently Reviewed*

"...proposes healthy ways to assess interests, skills, and personality traits while developing career goals."
— *VOYA (Voice of Youth Advocates)*

The Sex Book:
An alphabet of smarter love
by Jane Pavanel, illustrated by Grant Cunningham
▸ ISBN 1-894222-30-X

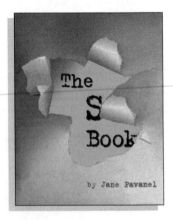

This non-fiction, non-judgmental guide for teens contains everything you might want to know about sex, but were afraid to ask. The handy A–Z format offers fast answers to crucial questions, dispels myths, and addresses the complex issues of modern-day sexuality.

"...confronts difficult topics directly and candidly..." – *Publishers Weekly*

"Whether teens are straight or gay, planning to abstain or to become sexually active, this book stresses informed choice through information."
— *CM: Canadian Review of Materials*

- Winner, Independent Publisher Best Juvenile/YA Non-Fiction Book Award (2002)
- Silver Medal, 2001 ForeWord Magazine Young Adult/Non-Fiction Book of the Year
- American Library Association Notable Quick Pick for Reluctant YA Readers (2003)
- Shortlisted, Norma Fleck Award for Canadian Young Adult Non-Fiction (2002)

Available Now!

...from the new Lobster Press Series, What's Your Style?

Let's Party!
by Alison Bell, illustrated by Kun-Sung Chung
▸ ISBN 1-894222-99-7

The latest book in the **What's Your Style?**
Series lets girls find original concepts for
get-togethers, discover more about their
own style, and celebrate special friend-
ships! With mix n' match party ideas,
quizzes, and personality-specific
troubleshooting tips, **Let's Party!** is the
perfect guide for any aspiring hostess.

Fearless Fashion
by Alison Bell, illustrated by Jérôme Mireault
▸ ISBN 1-894222-86-5

Fashion is more than the right pair of
jeans or a cool micro-mini; it is a potent
vehicle of self-expression. It is everywhere around us, yet elusive as the
perfect shade of lip gloss. So what is
style? Where does it come from? And
which one suits you best? Find out in
Fearless Fashion!

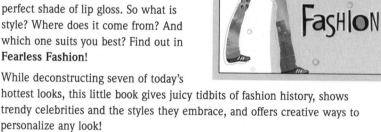

While deconstructing seven of today's
hottest looks, this little book gives juicy tidbits of fashion history, shows
trendy celebrities and the styles they embrace, and offers creative ways to
personalize any look!

"...urges teens to experiment and to keep in mind that style develops over
time, and that *The best fashion trend is to be true to yourself.*"
                                                                 – *School Library Journal*

"...[with a] positive message of self-concept, and self-discovery... This is a
great book..." – *Resource Links*